Chicago Checkmate
Chicago Secrets Vol. III

J. Thomas Ganzer

Cover photo shot by Mary and Maurizio, Amalfi Coast of Italy, for Flytographer www.flytographer.com

Cover design courtesy of Rachel Corpus of X Strategies https://www.xstrats.com/

Cover model Angela Navarrete Opazo, MD, PhD

ISBN 978-1-61225-387-9

Copyright © 2017 J. Thomas Ganzer
All Rights Reserved

No part of this publication may be reproduced in any form or stored, transmitted or recorded by any means without the written permission of the author.
\
This is a work of fiction. Names, characters, businesses, places, events and incidents are either the products of the author's imagination or used in a fictitious manner. Any resemblance to actual persons, living or dead, or actual events is purely coincidental.

Published by Mirror Publishing
Fort Payne, AL 35967
www.pagesofwonder.com

Printed in the USA

For Mom.

Acknowledgements

Thanks to many for making the Chicago Secrets series happen. For this installment, hugs to my editor Paige Prince for not strangling me, my betas Patti Fisher, Anna Kettlewell, and Mary Ann Ganzer for their time reading and discussing the story, and authors Angora Shade and Laurie Vincent for their constant advice and encouragement. And, as always, shout out to the hardworking staff at Mirror Publishing.

About the Author

J. Thomas Ganzer is an attorney practicing in Milwaukee, Wisconsin. He has experience in both civil and criminal matters in private practice and at the Wisconsin Department of Justice. He currently practices civil litigation for the Milwaukee Metropolitan Sewerage District. Armed with a diverse career, J. Thomas offers his readers a unique perspective on the traditional legal thriller, focusing on the odd characters and constant one-upmanship that lawyers, clerks, and judges know all too well.

Contact Information

J. Thomas Ganzer
jtganzer@gmail.com

Chapter 1

Government workers are, contrary to popular opinion, genetically identical to the rest of the world. Once they punch the clock, they spend their days climbing over one another in an attempt to become the crab at the top of the bucket, while the rest try to pull them back down a bureaucratic payscale. Over the last several years, Joe Haise clawed over the pile better than anyone.

Joe was nothing special, a federal prosecutor in Chicago handling white-collar prosecutions of those who weren't quite rich enough or smart enough to avoid getting caught. It wasn't glamorous and he never made the news, he just plodded along his nine-to-five gig, no waves made and no feathers ruffled.

His wife Tina was his pride and showpiece, his petite blonde arm candy. She ran a small nonprofit and she knew her place, which was at Joe's side. They maintained a small, discreet home in Libertyville, wore discreet clothing, and spoke in discreet terms. It was all so very appropriate.

The world went haywire when he discovered Tina led a double life as a professional—and quite high-priced—escort. Joe's world snapped, his psyche snapped, and Tina's neck snapped, in that order. Oh Suzanna, what to do, what to do? Joe did what any good prosecutor would: he hid the evidence, feigned his grief, and used the tragedy to his advantage to nail a promotion, one commendation, a patsy to take the fall, and a large wrongful death settlement to pad the ol' bank account. This meager civil servant discovered that murder and evidence-tampering fit him like a tailored suit. And really, why stop at just one body? Patsies are a wonderful thing, after all.

Oh, and what a patsy he was. Hedge fund magnate Gary Maxwell made the mistake of being rich, married, and occasionally fucking expensive ladies of the evening. It was never a problem before, but it was different this time. She was different. They clicked. She had a controlling husband, Gary had an ice-cold wife. He wouldn't dump his spouse for some whore he met online; the alimony alone would kill him. But for the moment, she was worth every penny as she was quite the professional, both in and out of bed. He might have even loved her. If not for impeccably bad timing, everything would have been jake. But her sonofabitch husband showed up one night and strangled her right in his damn driveway. Gary discovered the body at the precise moment a paperboy discovered Gary discovering the body. By the time the cops showed up, Joe was in the wind, Gary in the clink, and the press led the torch-bearing mob. But at the end of the day, the two men knew the score—Joe was a grieving widow, humble servant of the people, and punisher of the rich and criminal; Gary was a slick adulterer who killed his adorable mistress and disgraced his statuesque wife. Gary kept quiet and took a manslaughter plea, wrote the murdering bastard a big check, and prayed early release would free his ass before the cancer would free his soul.

And the world turned. Everything went according to Hoyle until they all fell into an unrelated case involving a no-name stock hustler named Ruby Lester who worked for Maxwell back in the day. This financial used car salesman unwittingly brought them all together before God and a jury of their peers. And there, on the witness stand with nothing to gain and everything to lose, Gary the patsy pointed a bony finger to the brooding figure sitting in back of the courtroom and called Joe Haise a killer. Joe vaulted the bar in a blind rage and dove toward the witness stand, but was tackled in the well of the courtroom. Paramedics were summoned to deal with a "…male subject suffering a mental breakdown." There, in the chaos of the moment, they all understood a reckoning was on the horizon. It was inevitable, after all.

Four hours later, the venerated prosecutor, Joe Haise, Assistant US Attorney and (self-appointed) Lake Shore Drive Lothario, lay strapped to a gurney in a torn oxford shirt and gray slacks. His Italian loafers were God-knew-where. He lazily tracked tracers oozing from the white-blue florescent bulbs overhead. The smell of disinfectant and urine stung his nostrils.

He endeavored to wipe his eyes but his body refused to obey the commands. He squinted hard and began running legal theorems in his head.

Expressio unius est exclusio alterius. The expression of one specific thing in a statute is intended to exclude all others. Post hoc ergo propter hoc. After this, therefore, because of this.

"Haldol is a hell of a drug, ain't it?"

Joe opened his eyes and made out the melted face of a colleague.

I know you. Who are you? You carry a gun. US Marshal. That's it. I know you from work. Work. I am a prosecutor, got it. Where am I? Fuck. Gotta shake this off.

"Guten abend, Hans. Can you loosen these damn straps on my wrists? My eyes are en fuego. Gotta rub the sandman out of 'em." Joe began to put the pieces of the puzzle together in his head. He recalled being in court and the feeling of four hundred pounds of men on his chest.

"No can do, Counselor. Big Man's orders. You had a hell of an afternoon." Hans looked like Hitler's wet dream: six-two and two hundred fifty pounds of Germanic muscle kept taut in a blue blazer, clip-on tie, and gray slacks. Joe recalled Hans as being one of the men near the bottom of the pile.

"No shit, Sherlock. Was I in trial? I remember being in the gallery for some reason."

"You were watching the trial. You had a little…mishap. Jumped the gate and tried to pummel a geriatric cancer patient. Not your finest moment."

The smoke began to clear. Joe was watching an old man testify. *Maxwell, that's it! Gary Maxwell. Customer of my late wife-slash-professional pincushion. All-around asshole.*

"Oh yeah, that guy. Hurled a bevy of unkind words in my direction. Can you imagine? Total breach of protocol, if you ask me." Joe plopped his head back on the gurney and tried to will the drugs from his system, lest he slip up and confess to something he most certainly did.

Hans laughed. "He said you killed your own damn wife, he did. Guy who did it now blames you for it. Thing of it is, Big Man is giving it some thought. Says he wouldn't torpedo his only shot at early release if there wasn't something going on." Hans tapped his breast pocket. "Got a letter here from him saying you need to steer clear of the office for thirty days while he does his due diligence. Paid leave, at least."

Joe tried to process this information. The narcotics felt like a sopping wet mover's blanket draped over his entire body.

Okay, just concentrate. I'm not under arrest, I think. He'd have a warrant, not a letter from Dunham. I gotta get out of here. Christ, if the boss thinks I killed Tina, I have a problem. I killed her, of course, but why is that any of his business?

Footsteps down the hallway grew louder until a slender arm reached in and peeled back the curtain. A twelve-year-old-looking male intern with a soft British lilt, hailing from what Joe could only guess was some far-flung Pakist-India village, greeted the federal prosecutor, now accused murderer, Joe Haise.

"Well, how are we doing Mister…Hay-See?"

"It's Haise, like…Hay with a Z at the end. And I want these damn straps off."

"Well, let us make sure you are not going to be raining blows down upon anyone, sir." The resident used a penlight alternating between Joe's eyes, checking for a reaction.

"And where are you now, sir?"

Joe bit his cheeks; the pain forced his concentration. "Judging by your age and shitty grasp of English, I am probably at Chicago Mercy because my boss didn't want to send me to a good hospital."

Joe gave the kid credit; he didn't flinch. "Very well, sir. I will remove the restraints, but if you try to assault me, sir, this gentleman will arrest you. You still have an IV in your arm so do not thrash about."

Hans nodded dutifully to the physician, who began unbuckling the cloth straps from Joe's extremities. After freeing his patient, he departed to fetch a nurse. Joe slowly flexed his arms and bent his knees. He needed to appear in control, as always. He braced for the feeling of steel on his wrist in the event Hans was under orders to take him in for booking. But no one produced handcuffs and Hans merely watched Joe like a zoo animal during playtime. Joe's tongue felt like sandpaper and he sat up and asked for a cup of water. Hans obliged, and within a minute Joe was able to read the writing on the wristband. *Chicago Mercy, Haise, J. dob 5/1/71.*

Okie doke, I'm here on a mental evaluation. All right, they can keep me here if *they want to hustle all the paperwork for an involuntary hold. Which they won't, so long as I am not ranting and raving. I am not under arrest so they will probably chalk up the courtroom outburst to temporary rage at confronting my $500-an-hour whore-wife's client. Killer. Whatever.*

Joe swung his feet over the edge and spent a minute pondering whether to stand. Hans tensed but did little else. Joe cleared his throat several times and alternated between balling up his fists and shaking out his hands. He ran his fingers through his thinning brown hair, the unrelenting stress of the inconvenience of being (accurately) accused of murder had wrought havoc on his hairline. He then patted his small paunch and silently dedicated himself to working out like a fiend until it was gone.

"Hans, I think I am good to stand. Can I get the hell out of here, or what?" Joe baited Hans with the question, working him to get a sense of what his orders were.

"Well, I gotta give you the thirty-day letter, pard. Then I'm 'sposda to drive you home."

Whew, dodged that bullet. Thirty days. I have thirty days to get this in order. Too much disorder, too much happening. Moving parts and so forth. Have to get into character.

"Yeah, no worries, Hans. I get it. That sonofabitch said that I killed Tina. In open court, no less. Can you imagine? Guess I let him get under my skin. Surely, the boss understands."

Hans piped up. "Oh yeah, Joe. Me and the boys were talking about it. Shit, I woulda smoked the clown if I was standing where you were. Or at least caved his goddamn face in. But you know Dave; he's gotta do something about it. Jackie Dekker, too."

Joe craned his neck. "Oh? Jackie had something to say?" Jackie was Joe's young protégé, several years out of law school and making some good strides in the office, under his fine tutelage, of course. She looked like an athletic fashion model and was virtuous to boot. Not at all a slut, like that bitch Tina was. Jackie had shoulder-length honey-blonde hair, bright blue eyes, and her legs looked great in a pair of heels. High arch, slender painted toes, and smooth, tan skin. A half-dozen pairs of her pilfered running socks adorned his bedroom nightstand.

Jackie was prosecuting a carnival-barking fraudster named Ruby

Lester when Gary Maxwell, Ruby's former boss, ended up being a goddamn witness. Of all the dumb luck. As far as the rest of Chicago knew, Maxwell was fucking a federal prosecutor's wife and choked her to death in a lover's quarrel. Her true profession never factored into it; it didn't do Gary or Joe any good to let that get out. A few years into his ten-year sentence, Maxwell parlayed his proffered testimony against Ruby into a shot at early parole. But he would've kept quiet about Tina, Joe made sure of it. Ruby's case was just a white-collar scam, after all, and a closed murder case shouldn't have been on the dance card, right? Then Maxwell went and blew the whole thing to hell when he frogged on the witness stand and said Joe killed his wife when nobody really asked him his goddamn opinion on the matter, anyway. Thereby fucking up the whole wide world.

Hans nodded. "Well, Ms. Dekker was in Dave's office for a long time and was pretty shaken up after the melee. When we led her out of the courtroom, she kept saying that you were half-scooters, so Dave prolly had to do some equal opportunity bullshit on account of her. You know how it is. They shipped that sculpted ass of hers down Springfield way. Sucks, 'cause she was nice to look at. Whatever. Thirty days and you're back in the saddle."

A nurse entered and greeted the two. She gloved up and prepared to withdraw Joe's IV. A moment later, Joe was holding his arm at an angle after receiving a small Band-Aid on the puncture wound. She gathered her supplies and slipped out.

Hans reached into his blazer and withdrew a crisp envelope. He handed it to Joe and stood up, gathering Joe's shoes and personal effects. Joe tore open the envelope and began to read a letter crafted just a few hours earlier.

```
Dear Joe:
I have been reviewing reports regarding the
incident in court today. It was disclosed to me
you were in trial watching Gary Maxwell testify
in the fraud case of United States versus Ruby
Lester when you vaulted the bar and attempted to
assault Mr. Maxwell in the middle of his cross-
```

examination. I further understand you were forcibly restrained by court personnel, nearly causing a mistrial.

I understand you naturally have great animosity toward Mr. Maxwell. Facing someone convicted of such a heinous crime against your late wife would cause anyone's anger to boil over. However, an accusation against you was made by Mr. Maxwell, under oath no less, and to his great risk since such an unsupported accusation would hinder his chance for early parole. Considering he had no obvious motive to fabricate such a story, I must give at least a modicum of credence to the accusation that you, not he, are responsible for the death of your late wife, Tina. I am doing this if for no other reason than to firmly clear your good name.

Therefore, I must insist that for the next thirty days, you do not enter the Everett M. Dirsken Federal Building for any reason whatsoever. You are also not to contact employees of this office, including, but not limited to, Jackie Dekker.

Sincerely,
The Honorable David Dunham
United States Attorney for the Northern District of Illinois, Eastern Division

Joe folded the letter and placed it back in the envelope.

Well, could be worse, Joe thought. *I have some time to get this situation under control and then I'll deal with that bitch Jackie.*

"Thanks Hans, let's get the hell outta Dodge."

The burly officer helped Joe to his feet and corralled his belongings. Joe signed the discharge paperwork and the two headed to the Sally port. A dark blue Crown Vic was parked in front, perk of being a Fed on official business. Joe declined Hans' offer of assistance and climbed in the passenger seat. *Better view here than in the back seat*, he thought.

That fucking bitch Jackie, she engineered this. Somehow. Maxwell was stuck in his little hell, riddled with prostate cancer and counting his days left on this mortal coil. All he had to do was die in peace. But no, he had to go off against me in court. He didn't even need to be there; he was a nothing witness against a two-bit nobody in a case going nowhere. Now this is a thing. A real, honest-to-Christ, thing. Gotta get ahead of this. I have thirty days. Dave is investigating, but if I can get ahead of this, he'll end up with a whole big bag of hot air and bullshit.

Joe leaned his head against the window and dozed off while the streetlights of Chicago zoomed by. He woke a half-hour later as they pulled into the driveway of his Libertyville home.

Chapter 2

Jackie Dekker, Joe's young, comely protégé, happily rode his coattails as he moved up the DOJ career ladder in Chicago. She could ignore his gaze, disregard his constant innuendo, and block out the stench of his dime-store cologne. After all, student loan debt doesn't care if her boss is a creep, and business cards with her name below the DOJ logo are pretty damn cool. A new boyfriend, a stable job, and no reason to rock the boat, she accepted the situation. But someone as bright as she is may only be kept in the dark for so long, and Jackie was beginning to see the light. As the bodies piled up, she could feel his presence all around her. Was Maxwell truly innocent of murder? Did her boss actually kill his own wife? And how does she convince people the boogeyman was real and worked in the office down the hall?

It was a hell of a day, which ended with a courtroom fracas when her star witness accused her immediate supervisor of murder. Which wasn't exactly a good thing to have on her resume. She suspected as much months before, but this was the catalyst she needed. Her lack of evidence be damned, no one could ignore what Maxwell did in court. Questions would be asked. Staff would be assigned. They would find something, *anything*, to prove he's a killer. How many bodies did he bury in his basement? But Joe Haise screwed up somewhere. She would just wait it out until they nailed his ass.

Jackie stared at the ceiling in the dark. She could make out a rust-colored water stain on the drop-tile square. It looked like either a large man's buttocks or two outer space aliens kissing. Or possibly one small blob consuming another small blob on its way to devouring the entire ceiling. Well, she considered it a fascinating stain, regardless. The Residence

Inn in Springfield, Illinois, in the middle of winter, is not the Drake Hotel in Chicago during the spring, but it is better than spending time with a colleague who is: A) her supervisor; B) a homicidal maniac; and who C) sneaks into her laundry to steal her damn socks. But considering the terrain in which she found herself deployed—being whisked away in the middle of the night, checked into a barely 3-star hotel under a false name, and reassigned from the bright lights and excitement of the Chicago office to the ever-present fragrance of manure in Central Illinois—this was a break-even lifestyle change, at best.

Next to her, snoring softly, lie her new boyfriend Kevin. Hopefully boyfriend. More likely than not. But definitely not a one-night stand; they had been dating for weeks. *I am not some floozy*, she thought.

She gradually became aware of a muscle pull in her lower back. It announced itself when she was making love to Kevin, but quickly written off as the result of knocking the sexual rust off her hull. But she knew that's not the case. Twelve hours earlier, she was forcibly knocked to the floor of a courtroom in Chicago and dragged under a table by her opponent, the revered defense attorney Jonathan Wickman, who probably was owed a dinner now for his act of heroism. She last saw Wick in Dave Dunham's office while the three of them were getting hammered on Dave's expensive scotch and figuring out how to fix a case when someone went batshit in the courtroom like Joe Haise did. A reasonable plea offer was made and accepted, and the matter of United States versus Ruby Lester was dead and buried. The matter of State of Illinois versus Joe Haise was just going into labor.

Jackie chalked up two murders to the esteemed Joe Haise, Esquire—Joe's late wife Tina, and a horrible first, and last, date of hers, Todd Perry. Joe spied Jackie out on a date with Todd and strangled him in an obsessive fit. But pinning either murder on him was going to be next to impossible. Maxwell, despite being completely innocent, pled out on Tina's murder to avoid a life sentence. And there was no physical evidence, witnesses, or even motive in the Perry homicide. The thought of Joe getting away with murder kept her awake.

"Still trying to save the world?" A groggy, muffled voice called out from underneath a pile of blankets.

Jackie threw an elbow in his ribcage. "How did you know I was up?"

Kevin rolled over, kissed her on the cheek and propped himself up against the headboard. Jackie reflexively cuddled against him and laid her head on his chest as he stroked her hair. Though early in the relationship, it sure felt like the real deal. She knew it, she hoped he did too.

He sighed, "Because when you love somebody, you know these things."

Jackie's heart stopped. She slowly sat up and drew a sly smile. "Did you just say you loved me?"

Kevin looked at her wide-eyed. "What? No. What? I was merely positing that, factually, participants in pair-bonding often become attuned to, ah, their partner's, you know, things and whatnot."

Jackie began to tickle him and mocked him in a singsong children's rhyme. "You said the 'L' word and you can't take it ba-ack." She kissed his taut stomach; as a bicycle path engineer and avid cyclist, Kevin's core muscle group was the stuff of every girl's fantasy.

They met by chance at a hotel during an engineering conference he was attending and where she was staying after interviewing Maxwell at a prison in Southern Illinois. Despite their relatively strict moral codes, they fell into bed together a few hours after meeting; fortunately, they had long-term chemistry which helped assuage the guilt of having a one-night stand. He had jet-black hair and liked to wear black-rimmed glasses that hid the softest, sweetest eyes she'd ever seen. He wasn't tall, an inch under six-feet. But she knew that most women looked at him and saw a shy nerd in baggy clothing. She knew one has to dig deep sometimes, and she discovered a diamond beneath his surface. She found something new and charming about him every day. Sweet, awkward, chiseled physique…how he was still on the market was a mystery to her. She settled back on his chest and shut her eyes.

"Mmm, nope. You said it, buddy. It's out there." She yawned and began to drift as the room grew lighter with the soft glow of a cold January dawn.

"So now that you can settle in at the Springfield prosecutor's office, what are they going to do about your psycho ex-boss back in Chicago?"

Jackie told Kevin everything over the course of the night. About

Tina Haise' murder, about Gary Maxwell being in prison for a crime he didn't commit, and about Joe's obsession with her. She told him that Maxwell was damn near a surrogate father to her and that she was going to get him out of prison or die trying. The meter was running on him and he deserved a taste of freedom before he died. The one thing Jackie held back was that Tina was prostituting herself and Maxwell was her client, not her lover. Gary Maxwell swore Jackie to secrecy and she would uphold her promise to Gary to let Tina's soul rest in peace.

The toughest thing was telling Kevin about the Todd Perry murder. She agreed to one bad date with a guy she'd just met at a time when her normally reliable radar failed her. Twenty-four hours after giving him the brush-off, his body was discovered lying in the street, strangled to death. Kevin remained silent and stoic, Jackie would not have blamed him if he said 'sayonara.' It was not fair to ask him to be with her when he legitimately could've been Joe's next target. But he took time to process the history and said firmly, "It will take more than that bullshit story to get me out of your life." They both giggled. Kevin believed every word and she knew it, but joking about it was their coping mechanism and Kevin clearly was not going to give up on someone like her so easily. Jackie tried to hide her tears through the laughter, but she failed miserably and sobbed in his arms as he told her over and over that he wasn't going anywhere.

"Your guy Dunham can arrest him, right?"

Jackie had to remind herself that not everyone's an attorney. "Well, murder's a state crime, so we—meaning the federal government—can't arrest him for anything. And as far as the State of Illinois is concerned, Maxwell already confessed, so it's not so simple. We have to find something on him and convince the State of Illinois to reopen the case."

"But he is fired, right? I mean, put it in the newspapers and call him a killer. Remember when Benson and Stabler did it in that *Law & Order: SVU* episode, and then the suspect committed suicide? Turn up the heat on this creep."

Jackie shook her head. "You don't get it. Joe just got a commendation from the Justice Department in DC for his years of service and he has an impeccable record. He was a martyr on the front page of every paper in the Midwest when his unfaithful wife was murdered in her lover's driveway.

There is literally no evidence of anything supporting Maxwell's accusation. Dave Dunham might have to give Joe his job back after the investigation along with an engraved apology."

Kevin let out a long whistle. "Jesus. So how long do you have before they have to decide whether to arrest him or promote him?"

Jackie looked out at the window as dawn lurked about. "Thirty days, starting yesterday. So really, twenty-eight days and a wakeup. He'll be in court as a defendant or a prosecutor, one way or the other. Can you believe that shit?"

"No, Jackie. I cannot believe that shit."

Jackie laughed. "Well, as long as I have you, I'll be fine. Mostly because you looove me." She reverted to a child's voice and began singing, "Kevin and Jackie sitting in a tree, k-i-s-s-i-n-g."

Kevin loudly cleared his throat. "Well, smartass? Do you maybe have something you want to say to me in reply? Perchance something along the lines of the subject matter that I recently disclosed?"

Jackie began floating away. "Hmm, I don't know. I'm kinda having fun."

"Oh, really? Do you want to do the cooking in this relationship from now on? We'd both starve, you know. Better rethink your position."

She was silent for a moment before the pain of the last month of her life, both physical and emotional, became evident in her exhausted tenor. "Kevin? Can you please just hold me for a while?"

He wrapped his arms around her slender frame, kissed the top of her head, and whispered as she fell asleep. "Love you, Jackie."

Chapter 3

Joe looked at himself in the mirror. *No, this simply won't do*, he thought. *Not for a federal prosecutor.*

Joe peeled off the bandages that covered his IV site and the various blood draw wounds. He turned on the shower and stripped down. He reeked of sweat, disinfectant, and shame. He'd made a fool of himself in front of his colleagues. In front of Jackie, of all people.

How would she sleep with me now? I was ranting and raving like some kind of a hobo. I lost control. That can never happen again. She needs to see the old me. The in-control me. Then she would understand.

Joe jumped into the hot shower and shut his eyes. The water poured over his face, washing away his iniquities and cleansing him of the disgrace of the previous twelve hours. The shower gel—Axe, of course, like the attractive and sexually active young men from the commercials—wiped away the black, rubbery adhesive from his arms and the dried sweat from his armpits. *Ah, much better*, he thought. *Time to plan.*

Maxwell accused me of murder on the goddamn witness stand. Fucker couldn't keep to our arrangement. I let him cop to Tina's murder and, in return, I don't squawk about his bullshit light sentence and settle a civil claim for an immodest fraction of his fortune. But then he gets called as a witness in exchange for some time shaved off. I agree to let him testify and not oppose early parole in return for a commendation from DC. And Maxwell understood that I wouldn't murder his cute ex-wife. What was her name? Veronica. Yeah, Miss Yogapants herself. Why is that arrangement so hard to understand? Quid pro quo, jerkoff. He probably decided prostate cancer would kill him anyway, so what's the difference? Now I have precisely thirty days to resolve this shitshow.

Joe had to determine whether, if he did nothing and just stood pat,

Dunham's little exercise would produce anything to corroborate Maxwell's accusation. If nothing new turned up, he would be home free. Joe determined he'd probably have to file a civil suit against Maxwell for defamation, or at least threaten to, if only to maintain the mourning and outraged widower routine. But since Maxwell went rogue today, there was no reason to go cheap now; and a million dollars did have a nice ring to it, after all. He considered his next move.

Dunham is goofy, but smart. But I don't think he'll miss a trick; if I leave it to chance, he might actually find something. Tina was my first murder, I am sure I made a mistake somewhere along the line. The GPS tracker I bought to follow her and that fucking kid who chatted me up in the aisle where I bought it, the burn phone I bought from that black kid, and a million other little lose ends. But not with that putz Perry, that was a fucking masterpiece. Not so much as an eyelash within five miles of his body. Serves him right for trying to defile a blossoming flower like Jackie with his loathsome seed. But I'm whistle-clean, that exercise was as pure as a virgin's panties. But I need to know what they know.

Joe leapt from the shower and dried off as he walked down the hall to the den with a towel wrapped around his waist. As a result of his efforts to surveil Jackie and Tina the last few years, Joe became quite adept at information technology, classified and unclassified spy gear, the deep web, and computer hardware and software. He fired up his desktop and opened his browser. On the surface, the computer was extraordinarily ordinary. Joe had no top of the line software programs, no additional memory cards installed, he even used AOL as his default browser and maintained a Hotmail account, all hallmarks of someone who really doesn't know or care about computers. He logged on, courtesy of his hippie neighbor's Wi-Fi account. That would be the irritating Dick Morehouse, a recent retiree that Joe loathed for his liberal sensibilities. If Dick put up one more yard sign supporting gay buttsex, Joe would burn his fucking house down. And if the moron kept an poorly secured guest account with the password of "guest," he deserved to be hacked. Besides, what the fuck was Dick's wireless signal doing in Joe's house? Trespassing, that's what.

Joe picked up a few tips from the FBI's Cyber Division while working an internet fraud case. Because his alliances required quite a bit of information and anonymity, the training came in most handy. Joe began utilizing an online program to spoof his IP address, basically changing the return address when he accessed a database. Because it didn't really work for a two-way exchange of information, he upped his game a few weeks back. He managed to locate a proxy server host in Russia, essentially a large server that would stand between Joe and the target. If the target initiated a trace, the IP address would not only lead back to the Russian host, but the IP addresses that identified Joe at the server farm hopped every thirty seconds. Joe's real IP address was somewhere in the river of thousands and thousands of other users, making it virtually untraceable. Even the best White Hats conceded it's a real bitch tracing an IP back to a specific address in a foreign country. Trying to get a foreign search warrant for the server in a non-terrorism case, and then trying to pin down the right user, was a complete fantasy. All of this presumed the user didn't use two proxy servers in two countries, which multiplied the problems by a factor of ten.

Weeks before, Joe began probing Jackie's personal email account in an effort to discover whom she was seeing. After her disastrous date with Todd Perry, and his tragic demise thereafter, she was probably keeping those glorious thighs clamped shut. But just because Joe could surf the net anonymously didn't mean he could penetrate a private account. That would take more time and effort.

Having logged on to his trusty Russian server, he accessed the US Attorney's external webmail account. Hoping the news of his suspension hadn't reached the HR and IT staff just yet, Joe opened his work email. Sure enough, his credentials were still active. The inbox was full with pedestrian messages about his active cases. No one had sent him anything about the meltdown. No media inquiries, no colleagues wishing him well. *They all probably don't know the news yet*, he guessed. The silence was good news, but also no help.

In a rare stroke of genius, Dave Dunham appointed Joe acting US Attorney for a week while he attended some events in DC. *His best personnel move to date, and perhaps a preview of things to come*, Joe liked to repeat to himself. Joe spent time in Dave Dunham's office when he accidentally-on purpose stumbled across Dave's email password. Joe tapped at the keys, and *voila*. The password was still current and Joe had access to Dave's emails. A few minutes of scrolling produced a goldmine.

To: Baruch Goodman, DOJ Office of the Inspector General

From: David Dunham, US Attorney, Northern Dist. of Illinois, Eastern Div.

Re: Joe Haise matter

Bingo –

Good talking to you about the complete goat-screw I have going on here. I have a written statement from Jammer Franks (his real name), the witness from the Kenosha spy sore. He positively identified Joe as the guy who bought the GPS a few weeks before Tina Haise' death, he recalls Joe mentioning it was to keep track of his daughter (he doesn't have any kids). Honestly Bingo, this kid comes off as a bipolar speed freak, so I wouldn't put everything on him. Detective Buddy Scott from Winnetka PD, originally assigned to the Tina Haise case, was here too. He likes Joe for the Tina Haise murder, but he didn't say boo when Maxwell went down for it. He also implicates Joe in the murder of a kid who went on a date with one of my AUSAs, Jackie Dekker, in some kind of Play Misty For Me obsession, but concedes he has nothing to back it up and the crime occurred in downtown Chicago, which is miles outside of his jurisdiction. FYI, Dekker is on loan to the Springfield office while this gets sorted out.

I assume you'll interview Gary Maxwell ASAP, he's got one foot in the grave and the ruckus today sent him on a downward spiral. He's cuffed to a bed in Northwestern Memorial. I'm betting he'll either recant the accusation—which is bad, or reaffirm—which is worse.

Stay tuned,

Dave

Joe leaned back in his chair. *Well, well, well, looks like the Patriots got the Bears playbook.* Joe hated the Bears, the fans were loud, boorish drunks. And the Bears were losers. The Pats were winners. Sure, they obtained information about their opponents they weren't supposed to, but they won. And wasn't that all that mattered? *Coach Belichick would understand what I am trying to do here; he respects men who take control of situations and enjoy the spoils of success. He gets it.* Joe logged off and considered his situation.

Goddamn Buddy Scott, just couldn't leave well enough alone. What am I going to do about you? Your case was closed with a confession, but you went and shit the bed. So what the hell can I do to limit the dam…aha! Hadn't thought of that. Well, that would help keep things in the proper perspective.

Joe laughed, pleased with himself. Exercising control over the situation pleased him. It is what men of power, like him, did. *Time to stop playing defense and start playing offense.*

Joe walked to the bathroom and removed the towel, tossing it in the hamper. He stood naked before the mirror, admiring his physique. Well into his forties, Joe was certain someone in such pristine shape, and with such important credentials, was entitled to a young, pretty lover. Perhaps even Jackie. *Yes, she could do quite nicely.* He slowly ran his hands up and down his frame as he became aroused. Others may have seen a potbelly and the beginnings of moobs. But Joe was certain women of distinction didn't see such things. He impressed them by the man he is, he was certain of it.

He snapped up a bottle of baby oil, dribbled a generous amount on his hands, and began applying it to his nude flesh. His chest glistened in the vanity light; Joe began shaving his entire body after Tina died. After all, porn stars shave their chests, legs, even pubic hair, and Joe had to be ready for such sexual adventures now that he was an uncaged beast. He'd mourned Tina long enough; the office would expect him to move on by now. Would he start with a ménage-a-trois? Perhaps a MILF or a Yummy Mummy. He could even sample a coed under the right circumstances. *What is the age of consent in Illinois? Seventeen, I think. Need to check into that.* The world was a plentiful banquet and Joe intended to taste the flavors now that his precious Tina was no more. He held his arms up to the heavens and moaned in an exaggerated wail. *Oh God, Tina! Why?! Too soon! Who could do such a thi*—*oh, right.* He laughed at his little joke.

Joe began to stroke his shaft slowly, admiring his manhood the way he imagined others would marvel at it, as well. After all, in the pornos from the internet, the girls can't wait to get it in their filthy whore mouths, the bigger the better. *You can't have this anymore, Tina. You didn't deserve this body. Your little whore-clients didn't look like this, did they? No, they were men and women of no standing in society, no discipline like me.*

He shut out the bathroom light and walked to his bed, peeled back the sheets, and climbed in. He settled back in the soft, king-size four-poster bed, one of Tina's final demands before her untimely, but nevertheless well-deserved, death. Joe reached over to the nightstand, rooted around the drawer and withdrew a single, white ankle-high women's running sock. He secreted it under the covers and placed it on his erect member. *We are going to have a wonderful evening together, Jackie.*

Chapter 4

Jackie arrived at her new office bright and early Monday morning. Around the corner from the building housing the US Attorney's office in Springfield is the Paul Findley Federal Building & U.S. Courthouse, a gray-white Art Deco style structure. The Federal court system in Illinois is divided into three Federal Districts. The Northern District is comprised of the Eastern Division, which includes Chicago, and the Western Division, which includes Rockford. The Central District covers mid-state Illinois: Peoria, Champaign, and Springfield. The Southern District handles everything from mid-state to the southern border with Missouri, Kentucky, and Indiana. The Central division is based out of Springfield, but there is a satellite office in located Peoria. Jackie's good friend Nate Washington, a former Federal prosecutor in Jackie's office in Chicago before he was appointed to the bench in Peoria, would be thrilled when he got news of her transfer.

Each US Attorney's Office has two main umbrella divisions, under which multiple sections operate—a Criminal Division (General Crimes, Narcotics and Gangs, National Security, Financial Crimes, and the Public Corruption and Organized Crime), and a Civil Division (Civil Rights, Environmental, Food and Drug, Civil Fraud, and Financial Litigation). Joe and Jackie handled Financial Crimes, though Jackie suspected the sex appeal of the caseload in the Springfield office was far below Chicago's. *No matter*, she thought. Jackie dreamed of being a heavy hitter in the world of white-collar crime, and Springfield was a step in the wrong direction if she still wanted that life. But after going through the hell that was Joe Haise, watching the politicking of Dave Dunham, the stress and lack of resources in that pressure-cooker office, she began to rethink her life plan. *Maybe a slower pace is just what the doctor ordered. Kevin is here, after all, what else do I really want? Or need?*

The receptionist in the non-descript red-brick building had just arrived, surprised to see a guest waiting in the lobby when half the office hadn't rolled in yet.

"Oh dear, can I help you?" She was a sweet woman who the nameplate identified as Mavis Anspaugh. She was at least sixty and reminded Jackie of her grandmother, right down to the bifocals dangling from her neck.

"I'm Jackie Dekker, a prosecutor from the Chicago office, here to meet US Attorney Rosalyn Jeffries. I believe I am starting work here today."

A look of alarm washed over Mavis' face. "Oh my, here? Are you certain? Because normally Human Resources sends out a twix about each new hire. Ruth? Are you back there?"

Before Jackie could offer an explanation, a woman roughly ten years younger than Mavis appeared and approached he desk.

"Ruth? This young woman is a prosecutor from Chicago and said she is supposed to start work here today. Name's Jackie."

Ruth also had bifocals and both women were now peering over the tops of their glasses at Jackie, checking out her clothes, her hair, even her shoes. She felt like a pageant contestant in front of the judges. *Miss Dekker, please stand here in this string bikini and tell us why you and your heaving breasts are opposed to nuclear war.*

"Starting here? Oh no, we would have received a twix about it."

I need to find out what the hell a twix is.

"I was transferred over the weekend from the Chicago office. US Attorney Dunham already arranged it with US Attorney Jeffries."

"Oh, I see," said Ruth, nodding thoughtfully. Mavis added an, "Mm hmm," for good measure. Now their interest was really piqued.

"Must have been a heck of a weekend to get you down here in such a rush," Ruth probed.

Jackie had to call an audible. "Well, I just go where they send me. Ha ha." The forced laughter was obvious. Jackie would make a lousy poker player.

Mavis shook her head in a show of solidarity with their newest colleague. "Oh, we've been there, honey. I got sentenced to nine months in Miami when they needed help prosecuting a big drug case. Took me a month to find a decent Baptist church."

Ruth threw in an "Mm hmm," for good measure.

"Oh boy, sounds pretty brutal." Jackie nodded and waited for someone to do something. *Come on, let's get the show on the road.*

But the three of them just stood there, the two ladies seemed comfortable in the silence. After an interminable pause, Ruth mercifully offered to take Jackie to meet the new boss.

"Well, 'spose we outta get going. Come on with me, hon. Jackie, is it?"

"Yes, thank you. I am excited to be here."

She led Jackie through a glass door after swiping a key card. Jackie was immediately struck by the atmosphere. At nine a.m. in Chicago, dozens of attorneys and staff rush about, meetings have already started, and people are sprinting off to court. The men wear power suits and the women dress to impress. Even the receptionist wears a skirt. Half the staff in this office, as far as Jackie could tell, wore open-toe sandals and khakis. Most of the men wore polo shirts and only a few wore ties. She could understand why many considered this a move from the big leagues back down to Triple A.

Aaaand this is where my career came to die.

She suddenly felt like fish in a bowl. The morning coffee klatches paused and people looked in her direction. Heads turned and necks craned to see the new attorney with a briefcase and a small box containing what they correctly assumed was desk fodder for a new co-worker.

The pair walked down a hallway to a large double door with wood plague bearing the description, *The Honorable Rosalyn Jeffries, United States Attorney for the Central District of Illinois.*

Wow, even in the middle of nowhere, that title is still damn impressive, Jackie thought. *The Honorable Jacqueline Dekker, US Attorney, Appointed by the President of the United States and Totally Free of Student Loans. Ah, dare to dream.*

Ruth tapped on the door and peered inside. Jackie could hear her ask softly, "Roz? A Miss Dekker is here to see you, something about a weekend transfer to our office?"

"Oh yeah, bring her in." Jackie heard a booming but friendly voice call out. Ruth held the door and Jackie walked in, closing it behind her. Roz Jeffries' office view wasn't as impressive as Dave's with its sprawling downtown Chicago view, but it was good enough for Jackie.

The US Attorney for the Central District rose from behind her desk. She was short, about fifty-five years old and heavy. But her round face broke into an inviting smile. She had a reputation of having a boatload of smarts, both book and street. Shortly after Roz was appointed, one of her male Assistant US Attorneys was arrested with a bunch of meth and a prostitute, which was bad enough. But the hooker had a huge swastika tattoo on her shoulder, compliments of a previous boyfriend that spent a few years in a white supremacist gang that folded as soon as the investigation revealed the leader was half Puerto Rican. An eagle-eyed citizen grabbed a screenshot taken from the hooker's Instagram account before it could be deactivated, a picture of the federal prosecutor making out with his hooker-Nazi-girlfriend, and it was glorious—sharp focus, sepia-toned, with a just hint of a bounce-flash. Annie Lebovitz would be proud. The press ate it up. Though Roz was new to the position and all agreed it wasn't her fault, Roz had kept a low profile the last few years to ride out the media storm.

"Jackie Dekker! The girl who bested Professor Jonathan Wickman and got a colleague accused of murder, all in one trial."

Jackie began to sweat. *Oh Christ.* "Well, it was really—"

Rosalyn Jeffries walked around and offered her hand. "Come now. I never liked that sonofabitch Jon Wickman, almost as much as I can't stand Joe Haise, so you got a twofer. Listen, Dave Dunham sang your praises, and he let me know about your problem. Not sure if Haise is crazy like a fox or just plain crazy, but you'll be safe here. Marshals have already been notified and they'll kick his ass if he crosses the city limits. Besides, I could use the help."

"That is so good to hear, ma'am."

"Enough of that *ma'am* stuff, call me Roz."

"Okay, Roz. I hope I'm not creating an HR mess for you, this was pretty last minute. The ladies out there said they didn't even get a twix about me."

Roz furrowed her brow? "What the hell is a twix?"

"I have no clue; I was hoping you could tell me."

The two shared a laugh and Roz offered her best advice. "Listen, things run a bit slower and a little less formal than what you are probably used to. Which means the folks gossip a bit more. So, don't take it personal when they start speculating about you. Word will get around by this afternoon why you were assigned here. Hell, the whole enchilada will probably get a write-up in the Trib this morning. A federal prosecutor being tackled in court after being accused by a witness of killing his wife is not exactly a common occurrence."

"It was pretty surreal. I haven't slept in a month."

"Well, you can get your wings back here. And the Inspector General will probably want to take a statement, I can't help you at all there, but you'll do fine. Ruth will take you to an empty office and we'll have you stop by HR and get you some credentials."

"Thanks. And I have found when I start in a new division that if I can put together a chart of the Financial Section's prosecutions over the last couple of years, summary of facts, result, sentence requested versus sentence imposed, et cetera, I will get a real flavor of how you folks do things here."

Roz smiled and nodded. "That's pretty good, hadn't thought of that. Ruth can call back the files for you; they would still be on site. Now get out of here and relax, you're safe now."

Jackie audibly breathed a sigh of relief and briefly considered hugging her new boss, but settled for a handshake and smile.

Chapter 5

Staring at the blinking cursor on the screen always made him smile. He loved the moment before hitting 'send.' Money was sitting on the other end, just waiting for someone to scoop it up. The name on the lease of the cheap strip mall in Charlotte Amalie, St. Thomas, read "Elias Manningford," but he could barely keep his aliases straight anymore. He is Horace to his family, but among the locals, he settled on DJ Elrod St. Delacroix, at least until he came up with something better or got a girl pregnant.

The US Virgin Islands didn't become US territory until 1917 when Woodrow Wilson shook down the Dutch government like the mafia, telling them that if they didn't sell the territory to the US, maybe the US military would just seize it to help fight the Germans. The Dutch, initially resistant to surrender the Islands due to the dark complexion of the native population and the US treatment of blacks in the early twentieth century, had a sudden change of heart. Twenty-five million in gold bullion later, cue the National Anthem.

Horace was closing in on forty; he was tiring of running low-rent scams, but he wasn't quite smart enough to devise a big con. So, he dodged creditors, victims, and the cops whenever he could, though the Virgin Islands weren't big enough to hide forever and he was developing a reputation among the locals as an annoying petty thief. Normally, being a lifer on the islands was enough to ensure their kin won't turn them over. But he was getting the sense his people were growing weary of him and his ways. He was one slight away from a neighbor ratting him out.

Though the Islands are a perfect seventy-eight degrees in the dead of February and the tourists do their level best to mimic the laid-back lifestyle they assume is native to the Islands, the locals know trouble lurks just beneath the sand. They show lots of smiles, but are quick to take advantage of the pigeons that wander too far from the resorts.

Horace abhorred violence and reserved it only for those who pose an imminent risk to his freedom. As a child, his grandparents would tell him they remembered a time when they were all Dutch and all had pride in their heritage, but the US government came along like a bunch of bullies and ruined everything, which was all the justification Horace needed to break any number of laws and still sleep at night. But the lack of a steady stream of income didn't bother him near as much as his reputation among the locals for being a really lousy crook. His peers mocked him as "Horace the Foolie" behind his back.

Horace had a rich, dark complexion, clean head, and faint goatee. He stood no more than six feet tall, but he wears lifts to appear taller and often compares his looks to Idris Elba, which wasn't too far off the mark. Women on the island got whiplash when Horace walked by, but by the time they got to know him well enough to realize he couldn't articulate any kind of actual job, he would be in the wind and they would be visiting their gynecologist for an STD or pregnancy test—occasionally both.

His office "staff" consisted of his morbidly obese second cousin, Stella. She favored bright, floral print Muumuus and sandals, and usually dyed her hair red and wore it in a short, messy bob. Stella constantly flirted with Horace, which repulsed him on several levels. But she's kin, which meant she would never dime him out to the police, complain about her salary, or fail to play dumb if the tax collector or a former girlfriend stopped by. When the heat would come down, Stella would help Horace close up shop and open under a new name a mile down the road.

Noah, Stella's uncle by marriage, was more or less a part-time employee. Noah was nearly sixty and couldn't be bothered to wear anything more than a grease-stained wife-beater T-shirt that showed off his paunch and torn Bermuda shorts. He was usually drunk and showed up only when he needed money or wanted to play dominos, but Noah was great when it came to strong-arming a debtor or firebombing a car because the vehicle owner needed the $1,000 insurance check more than they needed the ride. Noah worked for little money, mostly because he would forget to ask for payment after a job. But overall, it was a quaint little operation, which annoyed Horace. He had to graduate from the farm system to the majors.

Horace, who failed every grammar course he ever took, would have Stella proofread his missives, though she was even less educated than he was. She would usually make several corrections, confidently telling Horace things like, "You never capitalize the 'G' in government unless you are referring to one above the equator," which sounded just fine to him. Horace conceded to Stella that the reason the language in his missives was all kinds of wrong was actually inspired by another scam; and if it seemed to work for the Nigerians, why fix something that isn't broken? He reviewed his latest email, and its ten thousand recipients, one final time.

```
Hello dear friend!
     I am writing to which of giving you fair
greetings. Our mutual friend from the prior vis-
it has told me you are of kind heart and that
Jesus is blessing you with his bona fide love! I
am inspired to ask for your assistance in the
most personal matter, which is also PRIVAT and
cannot be violated due to International United
Nations Charter of Monetary.
     My grandfather is the lawful PREFECT of the
Virgin Islands, which the United States illegit-
imately purchased and displaced the Natural Law
of God. He is now being illegally hostaged in a
COUNTERFEIT PRISON in the capital and cannot be
applied bail!
     I am writing to you, as we are BLOOD RELA-
TIONS OF CHRIST and also Jesus. I am and have
been told by our friend that you are a gener-
ous human and may help to arrange applied bail
to release my grandfather. As he is the owner
of banking/bond house of Islands, he has access
rights AND transfer rights/duties of FOUR MIL-
LIONS ($14,000,000) of US, he can guarantee such
repayment of your help with also interest! He
```

cannot access this funds while he is hostaged in such CONTERFEIT PRISON.

Please send Two Hundred of US dollars ($200) to my paypal account (DexterJamely@hotmail) and you can receive back your kind gift with money interest AND ALSO blessings!

Your friend in Christ,

Dexter Jamely

Horace paused for dramatic effect, hovered the mouse over the screen, and clicked 'send.' He clapped his hands together and yelled, "It's done!"

Stella put down her half-eaten fungi, a kind of cornmeal dumpling that is a staple on the Islands, and applauded. "Yes! This one is gonna be good, guarantee that."

Uncle Noah, half-asleep in the corner on a folded chair, rousted himself enough to offer a thumbs-up and closed his eyes.

Stella beamed. "How much we gon' make, you think?"

Horace shrugged his shoulders and stared at his email inbox, half expecting a response to have arrived already. He declined to meet Stella's gaze and rubbed the bridge of his nose.

"Horace, all you alright? You don't look too well."

He sat in silence for nearly a minute. Stella tried to wake Uncle Noah. "Noah? Tell Horace we are going to hit with this one. Noah?"

Horace finally spoke. "We aren't going to get anything on this. I paid five hundred for these email addresses, they are supposed to be regular contributors to that Yankee televangelist. But I am tired of this, Stella. We aren't getting nowhere. I can't 'tief here no more."

Stella scolded Horace, which was unusual. "Enough of that, we made almost two thousand on those penny-stocks last month. This is way better than that. The message is dumb enough and talks all about God, so it is just fine. I'm certain."

Horace said nothing at first; he just shook his head slowly. "We need to get out of here, Stella. We have to go mainland. We need a big fish. I can't do this middling hack bullshit no more."

"Where you wanna go, Horace? New York? Miami? We can't start over there, we'll get eaten alive."

Horace folded his arms across his chest and stared into space. "Well, then we need to go someplace smaller. We need to be a big fish in a small pond."

"Well shit, Horace. Where the hell we gon' go?"

Chapter 6

Joe rose early, the ice-cold dark morning kept most of Illinois in their warm, cozy beds. A moment after the synapses in his spectacular brain began firing, he kicked off the down comforter and sat bolt upright. He'd recently read a spy novel that described the ability of the book's villain to rise from a dead sleep in an instant and Joe committed to being able to do the same.

Something about killing his wife lit a fire in Joe's belly. An ember had been there, perhaps his whole life, waiting for a breath of oxygen. The once-insignificant spark fueled him through law school and long nights prepping his numerous cases at the US Attorney's office. It even fueled his courage to ask a beautiful young woman named Tina out on a proper date. But when he discovered what his wife was doing with her time, offering her flesh to men and women for Biblical mammon, allowing a parade of men to pollute her womb with their vile seed, Joe snapped. She died quickly, with a look of terror and confusion on her face as he leapt from the shadows and strangled her in Gary Maxwell's driveway, just mere moments after Maxwell savored what had been pledged to Joe.

Joe rousted himself from a forty-year slumber. Murdering his wife for her unforgivable transgressions was the greatest thing that ever happened to him, he was certain. The spark deep within caught a breath of air and Joe chased it with a shot of gasoline. He prosecuted his cases with a fury unseen in his office. He left opposing attorneys gasping for air on the courtroom floor. He received a promotion, recognition, and even managed to help one of his underlings, Nate Washington, secure a federal judgeship, an act of charity that would certainly reap grand rewards in due time. It was as if fate rewarded Joe for his years of struggle. The insults and condescension from his own mother growing up, constant teasing by his college classmates for his preference for pursuits of the mind over drinking swill and supplicating himself for sorority sluts, the forced cuckoldry he endured as a result of Tina's desire to spread her filthy legs for money, it all came full circle. Now was his time.

But the clock was ticking and he needed to move. The Inspector General would be calling soon to arrange an interview regarding that ungrateful bastard's accusation in court. Joe would need to prep for that. It would be simple: deny everything. Joe had a case many years ago involving a tweaker named "Mainline" Marvin Jones. Mainline wrote bad checks all over the Midwest in an effort to bankroll a methamphetamine operation he hoped to run out of the trunk of his Camaro. A few weeks after securing the final installment of financing to launch his new business venture—several potential angel investors from the Chicago projects declined his sales pitch, forcing Marvin to beat a Pakistani shopkeeper with a sock full of nickels—the FBI caught him on the south side. They had him dead-to-rights on video handing over the bad paper in a check-cashing store, his fingerprints on the checks, and no less than six eye-witness reports identifying him as the fraudster. In the coup-de-grace, a co-conspiring ex-girlfriend fingered Mainline after she learned Mainline fingered her little sister. Mainline's response to this mountain of evidence against him?

"It's bullshit, dude."

And all of this because of Gary Maxwell. That little ungrateful fuck. After all I did for him, letting him bang my filthy wife in the ass, letting him keep some of his money after suing him for Tina's death, and remaining silent while he swung a deal for early parole. He could at least show some goddamn common courtesy.

Joe considered his alternatives as he showered and dressed. While he carefully styled his thinning wisps of hair in the mirror, his train of thought was interrupted by the buzzing of his cell phone. He glanced at the screen, which signaled a call from a blocked number. *Here we go*, he thought.

"Joe Haise."

"Mr. Haise, this is Special Agent Mitchell Farris from the Department of Justice, Office of the Inspector General. I was assigned by my supervisor, Baruch Goodman, to talk to you."

"Mitch! It's been years, how the hell are you doing?" Joe never met or even heard of this guy, but Agent Farris didn't need to know that. The two ran in close circles and perhaps Farris wouldn't be certain that they hadn't already met.

"Um, I'm fine, Mr. Haise. Thank you."

"It's Joe, Mitch. And I can only guess as to why you are calling."

The voice on the other end quickly turned solemn. "Well, yes. I've been asked by the Department to look into some rather serious allegations leveled against you by an individual named Gary Maxwell."

Joe exhaled audibly but stifled a laugh. "Can you just imagine? It wasn't enough that he murdered my angel-pie Tina—that's what I always called her, 'angel pie'—but he had the temerity to hurl a scurrilous allegation against me. He'll be hearing from my attorney, you can bank on that." Joe set the phone on speaker mode, placed it on the counter, and began plucking a few nose hairs.

"Well, regardless, I do need to meet with you to go over some questions I have."

Joe slathered aftershave on his face and gave his reflection a final thumbs-up. "Mitchey, my day is wide open. How does three o'clock sound, here at my place?"

Agent Farris sounded thrown, Joe wasn't intimidated or stuttering and his voice didn't waiver. This clown was clearly unprepared for a target like Joe Haise.

"That would be fine. And if you want to have an attorney present—"

"No need Mitch-man. I have absolutely nothing to hide." *Actually, I have a lot to hide.*

"Fine, I'll see you this afternoon."

Joe hung up, pleased with himself for titling this lesser being off his axis. He already set the table for this so-called interview.

Now, onto more noble pursuits.

He finished primping, dressed, and strode down the hallway to his office. Joe fired up his computer and accessed his offshore server. He opened his internet browser, clicked through his bookmarked pages, and spied his quarry. *A man has needs*, he would tell himself. He hadn't scratched that itch in far too long, and he would have been forgiven for selecting company in this fashion. A man like Joe Haise did not simply walk into some pathetic singles bar unaccompanied. *Excuse me, but did heaven lose an angel? Because I am referring to you. You are lovely like an angel. From heaven. Perchance to buy you a drink, turtledove?* Or whatever gentlemen said under such circumstances. Such people reeked of desperation and he would have none of it. Besides, for what he preferred, the fewer witnesses, the better.

A glorious soft-pink background covered the screen as baby-blue lettering came into focus. She was there, still open for business. *Still pining for Joe, aren't you baby?*

A picture loaded, filling the screen. She had shoulder-length dishwater blonde hair and the softest eyes Joe has seen since, well, since Tina. "Hot" or "sexy" don't apply to this vision; "cute" and "lovely" were more apt. She flashed a coy smile with dimples that could make a priest re-consider his vows. She resembled his late wife in so many wonderful ways. He opened the browser tab.

Hiya Handsome! It's Victoria. So glad you found me. I am the girl next door with just a hint of spice. I played three sports in high school, two in college, and I have the stamina of an Arlington filly. I have a husband and two adorable kids, but that doesn't mean a girl can't have a little fun, right? I have an MBA, working toward a PhD in Economics. I can carry on a conversation about theater, finance, and the markets (Blue Horseshoe loves Anacott Steel). And if you need gift ideas, Burberry will get you a night you will never forget. Where are we going? Alinea for dinner? Lyric Opera? I'll be wearing a black evening gown with a deadly slit up the thigh. Think I'll let you out of the limo in one piece? Think again! 375 roses per hour, four hour minimum. Can't wait to hear from you!

Joe drew a slow smile. *Such a tasty morsel*, he thought. He clicked the email icon and typed.

Hi Victoria! It's Jim and Tisa from Lake Shore Drive again. Looking forward to meeting you at last! Tisa has a real estate closing that Saturday evening, so you and I can meet for drinks around 7:00pm, she'll join us at 7:30p.m. The bar has a private room for wine tastings for select clients (I am as 'select' as it gets!), after which we'll adjourn to a romantic B&B a few blocks away on the lake. (If anyone asks, you are Tisa's college roommate. Ha!) I know you are driving a bit from the north side, but of course we'll make it worth your while. Have you ever sipped Moet & Chandon—

naked—overlooking the lake? See you in a few weeks!

Joe closed his laptop and surveyed the landscape. *Meeting that little strumpet soon. I have a lot of preparation to do. Plus I have that other matter I need to tend to shortly. And I have Ma-Ma-Ma-Mitch coming over in a few hours. Work, work, work, that's all I do. Alrighty Mitch, here we go.*

Joe began rooting around closets and opening drawers. He pulled an old Tupperware bin out of storage and unpacked its contents. He removed old framed photographs and lit a scented candle. He fetched the vacuum and began cleaning the living room. Though Joe ensured everything in his home was in pristine condition, a thorough cleaning wouldn't hurt. After several hours of work, he was ready to host his opposite number. Finally, he stood before his closet and carefully selected the appropriate outfit. As it closed in on three p.m., Joe checked his watch and concluded he was fully prepared. One minute later, the doorbell rang.

Chapter 7

Jackie spent the morning shuttling between Human Resources and her new supervisor, a veteran white-collar fraud prosecutor named Jeremiah Logan, though Ruth said everyone called him "Pops." He was a small man, barely five-foot eight, with thick glasses and a hearing aid in one ear. Jackie spent almost an hour with him as he pontificated on the law and his vision for Jackie's role in the division. He occasionally let fly a belch in between topics. Apparently, Pops was suffering some type of gastric distress that seemed common to prosecutors with thirty years under their belts.

God, what if that is how I end up? Lecturing to some cute twenty-eight-year-old lawyer while I pick lunch out of my teeth and expel random gasses from my body?

It was noon before she knew it and Jackie accepted an offer to join a few colleagues for lunch. Ruth, Mavis, Pops, and two younger male prosecutors bundled up and headed down the street to a Chinese buffet. Jackie reflexively scoped out the two men in the group—one was engaged, Vince, a handsome former minor-league baseball player from Arizona. The other, Jeffrey, was slim with dark hair and features, and was fabulously gay. Jackie realized she was lucky to have Kevin, the last straight, liberal, single man in Central Illinois. The group settled in at a large table and Jackie was ready to spin a yarn about an immediate need to deal with an unspecified security threat necessitating her abrupt transfer, but they knew more about the fiasco than she did. The universe of federal prosecutors was small, indeed.

"Now Jackie, what do you do for fun?" Ruth took the lead in dissecting their newest subject.

"Well, I played volleyball in college at Northwestern, so I play on the weekends when I can."

A collective "oh my" rippled through the group. Jeffrey seized the topic. "Northwestern? That's amazing. Were you any good?"

Do I really have to give my resume now? "Well, I was All-Conference. But I just had a good year; I don't think I was better than anyone else."

"Ha! All-Conference in the Big Ten. I'd say you were pretty good, my dear." Jeffrey paused to take a bite; Jackie sensed the group seemed to be eyeing each other for some sort of a cue. Ruth fell on her sword.

"So, Jackie. Did you really have a melee in court back in Chicago?" Ruth nibbled an egg roll as the group paused, eagerly waiting for their newest colleague to spill the beans.

Jackie swallowed hard and prepared for the onslaught. "Well, it was over so fast—"

Mavis jumped in with her two cents. "Now I heard that the prosecutor fellow had a knife. Raving like a lunatic about conspiracies and mass murders and so forth."

Oh Lord. "No, no. He didn't have a knife. He just hurdled the bar and charged through the well."

Pops adjusted his hearing aid as he wolfed down a platter of white rice and General Tso's Chicken. "I had a guy one time in court, he shat in his drawers and threw the whole mess at the jury foreman. Be glad you didn't see that, little lady."

Good Christ. "Yes, well, I guess it could be worse, Jerry."

Jeffrey went next. "I think it is fascinating. Far more than anything we have going on here. Central Illinois, honey. Our main exports are cow gas and gossip." He gestured across the table. "Gotcha some rice on your tie there, Pops."

Pops missed the comment and Ruth took the liberty to pick the grain off her supervisor. He smiled and thanked her as she patted his arm. The lunch went well past one hour and they all exchanged war stories. If this had been Chicago, the attorneys would be half in the bag already and scheming how to get promoted over their colleagues. This group took Jackie to lunch on her first day and made her feel welcome. Maybe Springfield wasn't so bad, after all.

The gang stood and began to get ready to go. Pops scooped the check and received thank-yous from everyone. Jackie decided to fish for some gossip of her own.

"Have any of you had any dealings with Judge Nate Washington in Peoria? He came from my old division in Chicago." Nate was a large, gay, black man in an office populated by conservative law-and-order types. Jackie was a thoughtful, attractive woman, basically a piece of meat in a den of lions. They clicked immediately and were the best of friends.

Jeffrey spoke first. "I did! He's great; everyone likes him. And he is bigger than any of the bailiffs, so the defendants all behave. He played football at Grambling, you know."

"Yes, I knew that. He is the sweetest man, we were all so happy when he got appointed. I'd like to drive up and see him sometime."

Vince piped up. "Oh, just go ahead whenever you get time. We don't stand on ceremony here. So long as your work gets done, no one pays us much mind. You can always find a reason to requisition a car and hand-deliver something up there with the clerk. It's just an hour drive, if you have a lead foot. He's at a seminar this week, but he'll be back next Monday."

"Great! Maybe next week, then. So if any of you has anything needing to be delivered there, let me know."

Back at the office, Jackie organized her new cases, arranged her desk, and texted Kevin. She already laid down the law that she would stay in the hotel until she found an apartment, assuming the transfer became permanent. Moving in with Kevin was not an option so early in their courtship. To emphasize the point, they agreed she would be out of his apartment by midnight during the week and two a.m. on the weekends, unless they were still in the middle of sex at zero hour, in which case all bets were off.

At half-past two, Jackie wrapped a call from facilities about a parking spot when the red light on her phone began to blink, indicating she missed a call. She dialed the voicemail service and punched in her new code.

"Ms. Dekker, good afternoon. My name is Mitch Farris, I am from the Inspector General's office in Chicago. I have been assigned the matter involving Joe Haise and I need to set up a time to speak with you. I am interviewing Mr. Haise today but I will be in Springfield late tomorrow morning and plan to stop by your office around ten thirty. If this is a problem, call me back. Otherwise, I'll see you tomorrow."

Jackie began to sweat. *I did nothing wrong, why am I nervous? What is he thinking right now? Is he panicked? Probably not. Does he blame me? Most certainly. He is awaiting a visit from a federal agent looking to bring him up on a couple counts of murder. He's going to be looking for some payback, sure enough. Just when I thought I left it all behind and could start fresh, it follows me here.*

Jackie decided she was fooling herself to think the interview wouldn't happen, that she could stay safely tucked away in Central Illinois and whatever happened in Chicago will straighten itself out. But that was naïve, and she needed to face the music. Just so long as Joe Haise was two hundred miles away, she'd survive. Literally and figuratively. It sucked being a grown up.

She rode out the rest of the day and texted Kevin the news about the interview. He promised a romantic dinner, a nice bottle of wine, and a foot massage would ease the stress. She said she would stop by after going home and working out.

As the sun set on Springfield, Jackie closed down her computer and headed out for the evening. Ninety-six hours earlier, she was in Chicago getting drunk in her boss' office trying to figure out what the hell just happened. Now she was stuck half a state away and living out of a hotel. Roz required Jackie be escorted in and out of the building for a few weeks until things shook out. A Marshal presented himself at her doorway at precisely five o'clock and they agreed it would be the nightly ritual. Half an hour later, Jackie was in her spandex on a treadmill in the hotel's fitness center. Five miles later, she hopped in the shower and prepped for dinner with Kevin.

Chapter 8

"Agent Farris, so glad you could join me. Please come in."

Joe ushered his would-be executioner inside with a warm smile. He could tell this particular adversary was not the sharpest knife in the drawer just by looking at his round doughy face and emerging beer gut. He was a carbon copy of most federal agents, rugged skin, high and tight haircut, and eyes that never stopped darting in every direction. Joe could tell Farris began to sniff the incense. Lavender oil is widely recognized as the most calming and soothing fragrance; ideally, Farris would subconsciously regard this as a positive interaction, and perhaps even conclude in the first five minutes that such a fine man could not possibly be a killer.

Joe placed dozens of pictures of Tina around the house—Tina on their wedding day, Tina on the beach, Tina with her pain-in-the-ass white-trash Schlitz-lovin' mother. Tina slipped her money from time to time, over Joe's objections of course. He hadn't seen her mother since the funeral and hadn't spoken to her since she called one week afterward asking whether Tina was insured or whether they could sue the filthy rich murdering bastard Gary Maxwell. Joe explained that, as her husband, only he possessed a wrongful death claim but that he wouldn't be pursuing the matter in court because, "Money won't bring her back, Midge." She didn't need to know about his confidential settlement with Maxwell and she hadn't reached out to him since then; she clearly was more interested in Tina's life insurance than her life.

Joe wore dark slacks and plain black blazer over a mother-of-pearl oxford shirt and no tie. The slightly ruffled shirt hinted at a grieving widower who could barely dress himself—Joe researched that—the dark clothes conveyed that he was still in mourning. Joe practiced looking somber in the mirror for nearly an hour.

"Let's have a seat. Care for some tea?" Joe poured himself a cup from a faux-British tea set that was a wedding gift but employed only when Tina felt the urge to pretend she was upper class.

The agent shook his head as he settled on the sofa. "No sir. This shouldn't take very long."

Joe took the armchair next to the sofa. "Well, my Tina and I used to have tea all the time. She was just an angel, in spite of her human frailties."

Farris opened a notebook and placed a recorder on the coffee table. "Well, let's jump to it. Obviously, you are not under arrest and are free to terminate this interview at any time. Do you understand?"

"Oh, I know my rights, Agent Farris, and I waive them all. Heck, I think I trained you on Miranda last year with a hundred others at a seminar downtown."

Farris shook his head dismissively. "Don't recall. Let's talk about your late wife. How did you two meet?"

Joe spent nearly an hour recounting their dating history, their wedding, and Tina's work with her charity that helped inner city girls spend a month in the summer camping and riding horses. He proudly recounted how he romanced her and, although she was beautiful enough to have almost any man, Joe conquered her heart. "And this was when I was a new Assistant US Attorney. Now that I am a Section Chief, I would think I could get… I mean, she would be even more proud of me."

Joe was always quick to point out how he paid for everything. "She didn't usually say it, but I knew she was grateful for my generosity."

Farris nodded, "I'm sure, Mr. Haise. Tell me about Gary Maxwell. When was the first time you heard his name?"

"When the police came to my house the morning after, well, you know. They took me to give a statement and identify the corpse."

Farris paused the recorder, fiddled with the settings, and set it back down on the table. "Now I'm here because Mr. Maxwell hurled some serious allegations at you in open court. Sounds like he hit a nerve because you went a little nuts. Fair to say?"

"Absolutely. I was not myself, that is for sure. Didn't appreciate his accusation, not one bit."

"Well, Mr. Haise, I have to ask. Where were you the night your wife died?"

Joe leapt into a prepared speech. "She was supposedly going to be with her mother down state. I went out for cheeseburgers, but spent the rest of the night at home."

Farris scribbled furiously but gave no indication of his thought process. "Mm hmm. Did you call her that night?"

Joe leveled his gaze at his challenger. "Now Agent Farris, we both know I did. I am sure it is in your file. We chatted briefly and hung up after exchanging 'I love you's.' I gave it no more thought. I can only assume, at that moment, she was actually with her lover, that other fellow."

"Well, Mr. Haise. That would really tick me off if I found out my wife was seeing someone, I'd wanna kill the bastard."

Joe bristled. "Yes, well, seeing as how I didn't know until after she died who she was seeing, I couldn't very well be upset about it, now could I?"

Farris furrowed his brow. "Whom."

"Excuse me?"

"Well, you said 'who' she was seeing. It's technically 'whom.'"

Joe began to anger. "Yes, I suppose it is, Agent Farris."

Farris casually flipped a page in his notebook. "Now, did you have any notion she was stepping out on you? Usually these things are preceded by a sudden disinterest in sex. Did you have sex with your wife on a regular basis?"

Joe exhaled hard. "My wife and I managed our relationship perfectly well, in all its forms. Why she chose to sully our vows with that *gentleman* is beyond me."

"*Gentleman*, that's a new one. If some guy was riding my wife like a rodeo bull to the bell, I'd find a different word. But let's talk about him. Maxwell, Gary Maxwell is his name. Do you have a tough time saying it?"

Joe was ready to fly across the room and choke this flatfoot with his own cheap Rayon tie. He spoke through gritted teeth, "I would prefer we not use his name in this household."

Farris nodded thoughtfully. "That's fine. Let's talk in terms of your late wife. Did you know she was banging that guy?"

Joe gripped the arm of the sofa and hissed, "Please don't use that kind of language in here."

Farris looked confused. "What, *banging*? What would you prefer? Fine. Did you know he was making passionate love to your wife for hours on end while you ate burgers?"

Joe began to turn red and spittle began to form at the corner of his mouth. "Now listen here, Agent Fuckface! Don't you ever say that—"

Joe caught himself; Farris stared at his notebook while he briefly fished around the inside of his sport coat, finally pulling out a handkerchief and offering it to Joe, which he declined.

"I'm sorry, Agent Farris. But that was uncalled for. Are we almost finished here? Because I am thinking you are only here to get a rise out of me."

"One more question. There is an allegation that you placed a GPS device on Ms. Dekker's car. What can you tell me about—"

Joe cut him off. "I did no such thing! I have no idea what you are talking about and I defy you to produce some evidence to back up your horseshit allegation."

Farris flipped his notebook shut and snatched the reorder off the table. "No, that won't be necessary. I have what I need. Thank you Mr. Haise."

Joe followed Farris to the door and burned a hole through the back of his head with his eyes. Farris paused at the small entry table next to the front door. An 8x10 frame contained a picture of a smiling Tina, arms around three laughing African-American girls standing beside a horse. "Oh, is this her? She was a doll, wasn't she? Such a shame."

Joe cleared his throat. "Yes, indeed she was. No need for her to step out as she did. Her tragic end was a poetic absolution of her sins, I suspect."

Farris set the picture down and rubbed is fingers together. "A bit dusty, though. Need to clean it up. Other ones look good though." Farris gestured to Joe's pictures of himself receiving an award, being sworn into the Illinois Bar, and standing in a group photo with his office staff.

Joe cursed himself. He forgot to dust off Tina's pictures after hauling them out of storage. "Yes. I will see to that immediately. Good day,

Agent Farris."

Farris nodded and walked casually down the walk to his car. Joe closed the door behind him.

Fuck, fuck, fuck! Motherfucker! Joe leaned back against the wall and slid down to the floor, banging his head into the drywall over and over. *Rookie mistake, I am better than that, goddamnit! A dusty picture, of all things.* Joe spent an hour cursing out loud, punching himself in the face, and stomping around the room. He expected more of himself than such a simple error.

First Dunham's email about Buddy Scott, then that little bastard from the spy store, and now Farris. Fucking Inspector General's Office. I can't believe this. After all I've been through. Well, it's his fault. All his fault. He's gonna fucking pay.

Chapter 9

Kevin's cooking threatened to derail any and all exercise Jackie sweat through every day. Sure, he cooked healthy: skinless chicken, steamed asparagus, green salad with almonds and a little crumbled blue cheese—because if we can't cheat a little, what's the point of living?—But Jackie had to question whether a second helping of, well, everything, didn't negate whatever it was she was trying to accomplish.

"Look, Kevin. All I'm saying is that if I want to attempt the Chicago Marathon this spring, I can't do it looking like a buffalo. So, can you make your food taste a little bit awfuler?"

"That's not a word, hon." He poured her another glass of white wine.

"Kevin, dear, are you trying to get me drunk?"

He freshened up his drink and they clinked glasses. "Hell yes, I'm trying to get lucky, here. In volleyball terms that you can understand, I am trying to bump a spike."

"That makes no sense, dear. Your volleyball-ese sucks."

Kevin's apartment was far nicer than Jackie's; dollars went a lot further in Springfield than in Chicago. They had quickly taken to spending dinners at Kevin's apartment. They would take turns shopping, Kevin would cook, and Jackie would clean up. Then they'd settle in for a movie or trashy reality TV. The conversation topic that evening was Tina Haise.

Kevin swirled the last of his wine. "So it seems like Tina had everything. Her husband is a nutcase, sure, but together they made good money. She had a nice home and had that charity of hers, so why throw it all away for this Maxwell character?"

Jackie had to tread lightly. She used her fork to chase a wayward asparagus crown around her plate while she thought of a response. "Well, why does anybody do what they do? She was looking for something that she couldn't find at home. And Jesus, looking at what her psycho husband did, can you blame her?" *Mmm, this wine is delicious.*

Kevin nodded. "Sure, she wanted a guy to make her feel good, wanted, appreciated. But the passion had to be part of it too, right? The seven-year itch, the steamy affair, the tawdry sex."

Jackie answered without thinking. "I suppose that had to be part of it. Think of the power she had. This guy Maxwell is worth millions of dollars and he turns to putty when she shows up in a lace bra and stockings. Having that much control over a man is intoxicating for any woman, especially some of the most powerful men in the country." *My head is simmering. Swimming, I meant swimming. Kevin is so cute.*

Kevin raised his eyebrows, "Even you, the very demure Jackie Dekker?"

"Even me." The wine gave Jackie a warm and wonderful burn throughout her body, settling in her hips. She waited long enough, dinner was over and dessert could wait. She stood and walked over to a confused Kevin, bent down, and kissed his lips. Her tongue flicked his like a snake as her hand slipped down to his lap. She gave his bulge a playful squeeze and massaged it slowly; she felt it grow under her commanding touch. Kevin began to kiss her back but as he tried to return the favor, she withdrew. The wine made her eyelids heavy, which helped her shoot Kevin a sultry look.

"*Tsk, tsk*. You want me to purr, you gotta know where to scratch."

Jackie peeled off her sweater and stood before a confused—but aroused—Kevin in black yoga pants and a white sport bra. She turned and walked a few steps away from him, peeled off her top, and let it fall to the floor. Kevin watched her disappear down the hallway toward the bedroom. He nearly broke the leg of the chair trying to simultaneously push back from the table and sprint after her.

Kevin rushed down the hall, pausing to strip his clothes off as he went. A shoe and sock, his shirt, pants, until he finally arrived at the bedroom to find Jackie lying naked on the bed, one knee bent and crossed over the other. She was propped on her elbows, staring at Kevin like a snake and offering her best come-hither smile. He rushed to the bed but paused when she held up a single finger.

"Slowly, now." She pulled him to her and he followed her lead. Soon she was on top of him as they moaned in ecstasy. The intensity built as they grew louder. Jackie was close, Kevin was closer. She whispered in his ear.

"Tell me you want me." Kevin repeated his orders with passion.

"Am I your naughty girl?"

He nearly screamed "God, yes!" at the top of his lungs.

Jackie whimpered as he approached the edge of climax. She ran her fingers through his hair and firmly grabbed the back of his head. "Fuck me, Kevin. Fuck me hard."

Jackie moaned as her man followed her instructions to a T. She was in control and he would have done anything she asked in the moment. With one final thrust, Kevin cried out. Jackie dug her fingers in his back and screamed. Her body shook over and over. Taking complete possession over her lover was a first, and the power felt good. It was as intoxicating as the wine. She screamed again as she let the passion wash over her body in waves. Their sweaty bodies intertwined as they collapsed, breathless.

After recovering the ability to speak, Kevin lolled his head toward Jackie. "Wow. What got into you?"

Jackie remained silent before offering a simple, "Mm."

"Yeah, but that was, like, really hot. What about the part where you—"

She was mortified. Born and raised in a conservative environment, she was not used to losing control like this. Screaming things in the throes of passion, acting like a porn star, it wasn't normal. It wasn't *her*. Maybe other girls did that; acted all seductive, talked dirty, but now she did too. It was out there, and he heard it all, and she couldn't take it back. Jackie hushed him through a firm whisper. "Kevin! You never talk about it afterward. Don't you know that?"

Kevin rolled his head back to center and whispered back, "No. But I know now. Wow, I am out of gas." He pulled the sheet over his body and quickly fell asleep.

Jackie laid in bed, staring at the ceiling in the dark. Kevin barely moved next to her, the wine laid him out. She thought about the last forty-five minutes, mortified by the things she said when she let her guard down.

What got into me? I'm so totally embarrassed. I never want to talk about this. Ever. If Kevin brings it up at breakfast, I am going to die. I'll leave. That's what I'll do, if he brings it up again, I'll grab my stuff and go. I never have to see him again, I'll recover. We've only been dating a little while anyway. Is this what Tina did every time? Is this what she felt? Shame and panic, a need to run for the door? God, it felt so wonderfully naughty in the moment. He was under my spell. I had total control over him. Ugh, now I feel like a whore. I want to go home.

Jackie quietly got up, trying not to wake Kevin. She silently gathered up the first bundle of clothing she found on the floor and slipped into the bathroom, slowly closing the door. She flipped on the light and breathed a sigh of relief when she saw that she managed to grab all of her clothes in one scoop. She quickly dressed, brushed her hair, and shut out the light. She stuck her head out the door and listened for Kevin's breathing. He was still asleep. Jackie tiptoed down the hallway, grabbed her purse and shoes off the rug, and snuck out the front door. Kevin had given her an extra key, but she knew locking the door would make too much noise. She jogged down the hall and broke into a sprint to her car. Jackie flew back to the hotel, parked, and ran to her room. Twenty minutes later she had showered, climbed into bed, and shut off her phone. Although it was after midnight, she channel-surfed until she found an old *Law & Order* rerun. In an act of muscle memory, Jackie pulled a pile of old knitting out of her bag. Though she hadn't knitted much since she'd started seeing Kevin, she took comfort in the ticking of the needles. Close to three a.m., Jackie passed out.

She slept for a few hours and woke late for the office. She flipped on the radio and sang along with Katy Perry, anything to preoccupy her mind. Dwelling on last night would've been paralyzing; she needed to keep moving. She decided against washing her hair, no time to endure the lengthy ritual. She found the need to constantly fight the urge to turn on her cell phone. She was certain there were a dozen texts and messages from Kevin asking why the hell she ran off in the middle of the night without saying goodbye.

Jackie hopped into her car and warmed it up; her phone was sitting in her purse begging her for attention. She threw the car into gear and drove out of the hotel lot, blasting the radio.

What is Kevin doing right now? He is pissed, he has to be. So what? I don't need him. I was doing just fine before I met him.

Drumming her fingers on the steering wheel, she began speaking out loud.

"If he ever tells anyone about last night, I will die. I swear to God, I will drive this car off a cliff. He better not."

She began gently banging her hand on the steering wheel, but quickly graduated to slamming harder and harder.

"Stupid, stupid, stupid. I barely know him. A couple months of dating and I act like a slut. Never again. Never, ever again."

She arrived at the office and checked her look in the bathroom mirror to make sure she wasn't a perfect shade of crimson as a result of anger and shame. She kept her head down and hustled to her office, shut the door, and settled in for the morning. But the intrusive thoughts became unbearable and she grabbed her phone.

Fine, screw it. Let's get this over with. I didn't need you anyway, Kevin.

Jackie powered up her phone and waited for a signal capture and the message alerts.

Signal…signal…got it. Messages…messages…sometimes it takes a minute. C'mon, let's go. Give me both barrels.

But there was…nothing. Not a single text, WhatsApp, or email. Her phone just sat there.

Well, what the hell? Is he dumping me now? Who the hell is he, anyway? I don't need this baloney.

Jackie turned her phone off again and threw it in her purse. The ringing office phone broke her train of thought.

God, this day cannot possibly get any worse.

"Jackie Dekker."

"Ms. Dekker, this is Agent Farris from the Office of the Inspector General."

I stand corrected. "Good morning, Agent Farris. I was kind of expecting this call."

"Yes, ma'am. I assume you know the drill. I should be there shortly, will you be ready?"

"It's fine. We can talk here at the office."

They said goodbye and hung up. Jackie prepped an email to Roz formally advising her of the interview. Jackie sat back in her chair and realized she was developing a spectacular hangover.

I'm gonna vomit on his lap and get fired. I need to prep my resume.

Chapter 10

Louisa Breckenridge was so excited. After her husband Gerald passed, she struggled to make ends meet. Gerald's pension with the union went belly-up and the monthly checks were cut by 60% and the gosh-blessed federal government didn't do anything to help. Social Security eased the pain a little, but there were plenty of outstanding bills and she skipped a few meals every week. Pride kept her from asking for help from her two daughters and besides, they had problems of their own and didn't need her fuss. Her modest home was practically falling apart, two cabinets in the kitchen fell off at the hinges and were sitting in a closet, but her daughters told her to take them all off rather than help to pay for a repair. "It is the style nowadays, Mom." The windows leaked cold air all winter and the heating bill was so high she had to pay in installments. "You should downsize," they said. Her washing machine would stick on a cycle, leaving the basin full of water that didn't drain. "Just twist the dial, Mom. It's a simple workaround."

    She became confused from time to time and struggled to remember certain things, with the exception of the hymns, chants, and well-placed Amens at Sunday services. Sending and receiving emails was very nearly the only reason she got out of bed each day. Louisa was poor, hungry, and more than anything, lonely. Until the mysterious email from Dexter Jamely arrived.

    It was confusing in the first read, but then it began to make sense. Our mutual friend from the prior visit…Louisa's friend Walter from church went to the Virgin Islands with his wife Marie last month. Walter must have met Mr. Jamely. She began to read the script aloud, offering commentary to her late husband as she read.

My grandfather is the lawful PREFECT of the Virgin Islands, which the United States illegitimately purchased and displaced the Natural Law of God. He is now being illegally hostaged in a COUNTERFEIT PRISON in the capital and cannot be applied bail. "Well, that's just like the so-and-sos in the government to do such things. They didn't even do nothing when Gerald's pension went south and didn't even listen when we told them how unfair it all was."

He has access rights AND transfer rights/duties of FOUR MILLIONS ($14,000,000) of US, he can guarantee such repayment of your help with also interest. "Oh my, that is quite a bit of money. I could certainly use a finder's fee, or some such thing. I could even have something left over to help the grandkids, Gerald!"

Please send Two Hundred of US dollars ($200) to my paypal account. "Dear dear, if only I had two hundred dollars, I would certainly send it to this poor soul. He doesn't even know English very well and yet he is trying to improve himself through faith!"

Louisa was excited, she could barely contain herself! She saw a fine young man trying so hard to help his family, if only she could do something to help his grandfather. She fixed herself some tea, though she took longer than usual as she forgot where she kept the darn things. *The whatchamacallits. Teabags.* Louisa sat and spent nearly two hours typing a response. Someone of such good moral fiber deserved her encouragement in his quest.

```
Dear Mr. Jamely:
Bless your soul! My late husband Gerald was
also a victim of the US Government and even
though we paid all those taxes, they never helped
us out! They will get their comeuppance on Judg-
ment Day, that's for certain!
I would send you $200 if only I had the mon-
ey, but I have to put everything I have into my
home to keep it maintained. Family is not able
to help out with the day-to-day like my Gerald,
so I have a full-time job just doing my fixes. If
you ever come to Springfield, Illinois, be sure
```

to stop by. We would have a pleasant visit, of that I am sure! You can even look at these darn kitchen cabinets that are falling apart while I prepare tea. Please accept my blessings, I will let Walter and Marie know I heard from you, they really enjoyed their trip!

    Yours in Christ,
    Louisa Breckenridge

She finished her tea, smiled at the thought of her good deed, and clicked 'send.' *I'll have to include Mr. Jamely in my prayers tonight,* she thought.

***

Horace nearly spit out his beer when he received his first response from his newest scam. He doubled checked his Paypal hourly, but he had yet to receive a penny. But the personal email response gave him the first glimmer of hope in weeks. He held a domino tile in his hand and pivoted to the laptop.

"Horace, whatcha doin'? We have a game here." Uncle Noah guzzled his beer and scooped another from the cooler.

"Hold on, I have something here." Horace read carefully, digesting every word. For Noah's benefit, Horace read aloud.

"Bless your soul…blah blah…Judgment Day…blah blah…have to put everything I have into my home…blah blah…Walter and Marie, whoever the hell they are."

"Any money in this one, Horace?"

"No, no money."

"Good, let's get back to the game."

Horace stared at the screen; he could see another message in the email. *Family is not able to help out with the day-to-day…If you ever come to Springfield, Illinois, be sure to stop by and visit…look at these darn kitchen cabinets.*

Horace considered this carefully. He quickly surmised this woman had no money and was older than Methuselah, but she was a widow, which meant she was lonely. She mentioned broken cabinets, so she needed help. And she had her own home, which might be worth something. But most importantly, she needed him. And he needed out. In the last week, no less than four people were looking for Horace—a process server, a fire inspector, a very pregnant woman, and her very pissed-off husband.

Yes indeed, he needed to consider this carefully. Noah and Stella were kin, sort of. But last week Stella, in a transparent bid to seduce Horace, asked him to check a mole on her thigh, which nearly caused Horace to vomit. And Noah was too hungover to steal a car for someone that owed a bookie two grand and decided to offer his car and collect on the theft claim from his insurance company. For Horace, he had too much baggage and it was time to split. Louisa Breckenridge was just what the doctor ordered.

"Hold your water, Noah. Hafta write something first."

```
My dear Louisa –
So glad you we found each other! I just re-
turned from services and I prayed I would find a
kindred spirit, looks like my prayers have been
answered!
    I no longer need your money, I am happy to
say my Grandfather has been released. Praise
God! I shall be in Springfield in two weeks on
business, I would love to stop by and visit! I
am also very handy and could fix your cabinets and
anything else you need. I would accept no money,
it is my Christian duty to do so. Please forward
your address and I will stop by with my tools.
    Your friend and son in Christ,
    Dexter Jamely

    p.s. Glad Walter and Marie enjoyed the Is-
lands, they had so much fun I doubt they'd even
remember me! Best not to remind them, I don't
want them embarrassed if they do not recollect
```

```
our chance encounter. I will pray for them too.
```

He paused while he considered the implications of his message. *Am I ready to leave? This is my home. Can I stay? No, no I cannot. I have to go. Wherever Springfield, Illinois is, I am going.*

Horace clicked 'send,' smiled, and returned to the game.

"Noah, what say we order some food?"

Chapter 11

Planning a murder is like litigating a case. Start with the end objective and work backward. Then plan every problem, every question, anticipate every possible answer, and then plan the next question based on every possible response. White pawn to king's knight 4, black pawn to king's 4, white pawn to king's bishop 3, black queen to king's rook 5. Checkmate.

Joe knew his prey, and he knew where he needed to be to engage the target. In case anyone asked Joe where he was at that fateful moment, he needed an alibi. In an ideal situation, a suspect would be accused of murdering someone with whom they have no connection, thereby eliminating a motive. Killing a random stranger in some town five hundred miles away when the wife would swear the suspect was sleeping in bed next to her is the gold standard of murder with an alibi and no motive.

But video cameras were everywhere and Joe wasn't killing some random victim, making it all the more difficult to pull off. It would be a challenge, but outsmarting the smartest people in the room was the only thing worth living for. Joe knew the feeling of having command over life and death. He'd been to Jackie's apartment building, he'd seen the drunken eyes of Todd Perry look at him in confusion before they rolled over one last time, and he saw the shock in Tina's eyes when he jumped her slinking out of Maxwell's house in the middle of the night. Joe pitied those who did not dare mighty things. Teddy Roosevelt was right, "they live in a gray twilight that knows not victory nor defeat."

Because motive was going to be established, an alibi became all the more valuable. Joe needed to be someplace on Saturday night for two hours. He fired up the computer and logged in to a local server. A few clicks, a credit card, the hum of his desktop printer, and he was set. Then he logged off and back on with Dick Morehouse's Wi-Fi. A bit of internet research and the image of his target appeared on screen. This was a person he dealt with before, but this time he was prepping for it to be the last. He typed a few words and waited.

Hey! It's me, still would love to meet, do you have time Saturday night?

The wait was unbearable, but Joe controlled his breathing. Panic was for fools. A ding signaled a response.

Hells ya! See you at 9:00! You know where.

Joe replied with a smiley face and logged off. He scooped up his car keys and headed out. He was going to be quite busy. He headed north through traffic until he reached the enclave of Lake Forest, a well-to-do suburb north of Chicago. A local theater called The Citadel put on productions there, mostly acts that couldn't draw what downtown Chicago would, but the venue had been described by the Trib as "charming" and "intimate." That particular week, they were featuring a piece of experimental theater that revolved around an actor and actress playing unborn twins in the body of an Italian housewife, pregnant by her Orthodox Jewish husband. The total trainwreck was called 'Womb For Two,' and apparently it was a musical. The thought of it made Joe nauseous. He parked and checked himself in the mirror. He pulled the bill of a cap down over his eyes, flipped up the lapel on his jacket, and stepped out of the car.

Anyone in the area would have seen a non-descript man briskly walking up to a set of glass doors, slipping inside, and strolling over to a sign that read "Box Office."

A disinterested young girl asked if she could help, the face behind the cap nodded, produced two $20 bills, and muttered in a gruff voice, "Two for Friday," as he pointed to the theater map to the seats he wanted. Two tickets spit out of the machine and the clerk handed them and the receipt to the stranger whose face she couldn't quite make out. The man nodded and disappeared out the door.

Joe made it back to his car and quickly headed back home. He placed the tickets next to the printer in his den, on top of a piece of paper bearing similar markings of the single ticket he bought online an hour ago.

He smiled as he envisioned the pieces moving around the board.

Chapter 12

Jackie convinced Mavis to put her in a conference room just off the lobby; she didn't need to be seen chatting up someone from the IG's office. She began to sweat as the clock ticked down. At one minute before ten thirty, her phone rang.

"Jackie? It's Mavis. Your ten-thirty appointment is here, I put him in the conference room."

Jackie, sighed, thanked her, and composed herself. Her headache was in full force and she swore to God and the heavens that she would never drink wine again. At least not that much wine, no reason to be irrational about it. She walked out to the lobby and spied Mavis gesturing down the hall. Jackie nodded and continued past reception to the conference room. A stern, stocky man was waiting.

"Ms. Dekker, Special Agent Mitchell Farris from the Department of Justice, Office of the Inspector General." He produced an ID before she could shake his hand, he didn't appear to Jackie to be the jovial type.

He didn't Mirandize Jackie; she wasn't a suspect. He simply pulled out a recorder and began asking questions. It was conversational at first, asking about her time in Chicago, Joe's habits, his behavior after Tina died. After thirty minutes, the conversation shifted to the murders.

"Ms. Dekker, you were there in court when Mr. Maxwell accused Joe Haise of murder. Did you know he was going to do that?"

Jackie began to feel flush, her alabaster skin made even the slightest tinge of red appear crimson. "I had no idea at all; I was as shocked as anyone."

"You met with him a number of times before he testified, and he never mentioned he was going to do that? Under oath, no less?"

"Swear to God, I had no idea. Honestly, I was hoping to get him on and off the stand alive. He can't have much time left, cancer is killing him."

"Yes, I understand that. I'll be meeting with him as soon as he is up to it. When did you first meet Detective Buddy Scott?"

Jackie swallowed hard. "Well, I began to suspect Joe killed his wife just because of how he behaved around me and the other staff, and contrasted that with how Maxwell acted every time I interviewed him. I didn't buy Maxwell as a killer. But it seemed like so much nonsense until Todd Perry was found dead. I suspected that Joe must have seen me with him and went crazy, so I put two and two together. Then I found a tracking device under my car, so I took it all to Detective Scott just to see what he thought."

"Well, the device under your car, Ms. Dekker, does appear to be from the area and we are talking to potential witnesses that could support your allegation. But why would Mr. Haise LoJack your car and then go nuts after seeing you on a date?" Farris' tone revealed doubt over her allegation.

Jackie exhaled, she felt like a prizefighter that can't keep their guard up and are being pummeled. "Because he is obsessed with me. He is always staring at me, touching me, commenting on my shoes or feet or toes. He tells me what to wear and tries to get me to talk about my dating life and sex habits and stuff. He is a possessive freak and I want him to leave me the hell alone."

"So you presented this story to get away from him and transferred here."

"Yes. I mean, no! Wait, what are you saying?" Jackie could tell she raised her voice too much, her colleagues must have heard that outburst.

Farris replied calmly. "Nothing Ms. Dekker, just asking questions. Now, do you have any evidence Mr. Haise murdered his wife or your boyfriend, Mr. Perry?"

Jackie cringed. "He wasn't my boyfriend, it was one date and it was awful. And no, I can't prove anything."

Farris became stern. "I deal with people facing ruined reputations every day, Ms. Dekker. Frankly, I see your fingerprints all over this courtroom debacle and I haven't seen one shred of evidence to back up your allegations of murder. This boils down to your theory that your old boss thought you're attractive and he may or may not have LoJacked your car. Can you see why this is a problem?"

Jackie began to regret ever opening her mouth. She hung her head as a sharp pain stabbed behind her eyes. "Yes, I suppose I see your point."

"Very well. I'll complete my report shortly. And if you left anything out or said anything to me that is false, I'll be back for a very different conversation."

Farris flipped his notebook closed and shut of the recorder. He curtly said he would be in touch and found his way to the door. Jackie sat alone until she was sure he left the building. She stood and walked down the hall to the restroom. She thanked the stars it was empty as she walked into a stall, locked it behind her, knelt on the tile floor, and threw up in the commode.

Chapter 13

Friday night came around and Joe was more than prepared. He spent the day driving to novelty stores buying little items to wear to the theater. A fake moustache, a little gray brush-in hair dye and a gray Tam 'o' shanter hat. Joe spent hours in front of the mirror completing his look.

Studies have shown certain things can render a subject invisible. Joe studied these psychological tricks of the trade for years in seminars and training sessions. Eyewitness testimony has gradually moved from the best evidence there is to the most unreliable. Own-race bias refers to witnesses having trouble differentiating between similar-looking subjects of a different race, the so-called "they all look alike to me" dynamic. In nearly 70% of the cases of DNA being used to free an innocent prisoner, there was an eyewitness who positively identified the wrong guy in court.

Witnesses also tend to focus on one stark characteristic to the exclusion of all others. A witness seeing a subject with a bright red cap might ignore the fact that the subject had a birthmark under his eye. Noticing the birthmark means they missed the earring, and so on. Joe needed to be remembered and forgotten in the same instant.

The moustache was expensive; Joe scored it from a party and costume store on the far south side. He stayed bundled up in the store, the brisk morning made that easy. The clerk could see nothing but a scarf and cold two blue eyes peering out and Joe paid cash. He bought the hair dye at a small drug store and a trip to Goodwill offered the rest of the ensemble.

He checked his watch, an hour to curtain. He grabbed his new but gently-used overcoat and scarf, took a deep breath, and headed out for the night. He drove east and south for five miles, occasionally turning down a side street and reemerging a few blocks away. He eventually found an old church nearly a mile away and pulled into the back of the darkened parking lot. He braced himself for the cold wind, climbed out, and began the walk to the theater. Cars whipped by the solitary figure lumbering along the road, but no one stopped to offer a ride in the freezing night. Chicago's indifference to a lone pedestrian was something Joe was counting on. He arrived exactly on time, eight minutes to curtain. He walked through the parking lot and, after checking for onlookers, peeled off his topcoat, and stuffed it under an SUV. No need to make contact with the coat check girl. But he kept the scarf wrapped around his neck and the hat pulled down over his eyes. A small crowd filed in through the glass doors, Joe casually strolled in behind them and approached the ticket-taker. He steadied himself, he never worked to be invisible before and all the research in the world couldn't prepare him for this moment. He felt a drop of sweat drip down his face in spite of the winter bite, the change in temperature combined with the perspiration made the glue on his face begin to fail.

Please God, just hang on a few more minutes.

The aged female usher, not very attractive and a little on the heavy side as far as Joe was concerned, reached out her arm and looked at her customer. "Ticket please."

She nodded to the lone patron in front of her; he didn't seem the talkative type. She noted he wore one of those old-fashioned hats that Irish guys had in the movies, sported wisps of gray hair on the temples and eyebrows, and had an almost cartoonishly bushy mustache. He wore a scarf around his neck, it rested against a dark turtleneck and dark gray blazer. A gloved hand offered an actual ticket from the box office, so many use the darned internet to purchase tickets these days.

"Seat 6, all the way in the back at the end. Enjoy the show."

The man mumbled some kind of acknowledgment and moved on while she looked at the next guests, a handsome young couple that reminded her of her daughter and the wonderful young man she was seeing. She quickly forgot the quiet older man with the bushy mustache.

Joe selected his spot carefully, back row, last seat. The one next to him remained empty, he made sure of that when he bought the extra ticket and discarded it. With no one next to him, he quickly pulled out his cell phone and feigned interest in the screen to avoid eye contact. Shortly after he sat, the lights dimmed and the curtain rose. A pair of voices sang as the lights came up, revealing two actors in nude body stockings signing to each other.

"We are two of a kind, blessed by the Lord. Sharing this womb, and this umbilical cord...."

Sweet Jesus, I'd rather go to prison than sit here for two hours. Murder is such an ugly affair.

Joe forced himself to stay awake and paid attention to every awful moment of the play. After all, he is supposed to be here tomorrow night.

One hour and fifty-nine minutes later, the audience stood and clapped as the final note played. As soon as the rear doors opened, Joe waited for the first members of the crowd to file out. He drifted behind them and kept his eyes down as he hit the doors. He looked back over his shoulder out of reflex and locked eyes with someone, the woman who took his ticket. She saw him only briefly, but Joe's blood ran cold. In that instant, he was certain she saw right through him, through his disguise.

He turned and hustled out. He jogged ahead to the SUV and reached under the car, scooped up his coat off the ground, and began briskly walking the mile hike to his car. He climbed in, blasted the heater, and peeled out of the lot. Half an hour later, he made it to the back of a parking lot of a restaurant that closed up an hour earlier. He ripped off his disguise and thrift store clothes, hat and jacket, tossed them into a garbage bag and tossed it into the Dumpster. This particular business had Saturday morning pickup and his disguise would be under a pile of landfill in twenty-four hours.

He threw on his jacket, sped home, and ran inside; his adrenaline was pumping and he felt the exhilaration that only came with the power he exuded over another. The game was afoot and he was on a euphoric high. He stripped and threw his clothes in the laundry, then jumped in the shower. *Can't be too safe*, he thought.

He dried off and smiled from ear to ear as he fired up the computer and, after borrowing his neighbor's Wi-Fi and his Russian internet provider, logged into Dave Dunham's email. To his surprise, there was an email from Special Agent Mitch Farris.

Well, well, what have you found, you nosy little fuck?

Joe opened the email and devoured its contents.

To: David Dunham, US Attorney, Northern Dist. of Illinois, Eastern Div.
From: SA Mitchell Farris, OIG Investigation Division
Cc: Baruch Goodman, DOJ Office of the Inspector General
Re: Joe Haise matter

US Attorney Dunham –

Per your request, this is a brief status report on my investigation, I am cc'ing my supervisor in Washington. A formal and complete report will follow when I conclude my investigation.

Gary Maxwell – Mr. Maxwell is still recovering but he should be ready for an interview tomorrow.

Jacqueline Dekker – I interviewed Ms. Dekker, she appears to be sincere in her beliefs and a credible witness. However, she has no concrete evidence to offer and may not be of value in determining whether Mr. Haise is guilty of any offense. Placing the LoJack under her car, if it can be tied to Mr. Haise, is a criminal act but may be the extent of the case. Her supervisor, US Attorney Rosalyn Jeffries, reports Ms. Dekker has adjusted well and her coworkers have taken a shine to her. You may want to consider making her temporary assignment a permanent one.

Joseph Haise – I interviewed him at his house. The living room looked like some contrived shrine, reminds me of when the jury did a viewing of OJ's house – fresh-cut flowers, pictures of his late wife, and some nausea-inducing potpourri. He used the word 'me' 29 times, used his wife's name precisely once, coldly recalled identifying her 'corpse' (in 25 years, I've never heard a grieving widower use that word in reference to their dead spouse), and seemed to imply he could land an even better woman now. He also showed a flash of temper that literally caused me to reach inside my jacket and unfasten my Glock. I am still gathering evidence, but he is dirty. I'd bet my life on it.

Joe's face went pale and he fell back in his chair. His heart began to race and he became dizzy.

No. No no no. Christ, I am so close. He isn't going to burn me. No way, not this chump. "You'd bet your life on it?" You just did, you little fuck.

Joe logged off. He stood and threw his chair across the room. He screamed and punched the doorjamb over and over until his knuckles bled. He finally collapsed in exhaustion and on the verge of hyperventilating. Joe needed an outlet for his rage, tomorrow night he'd find it. He couldn't wait to make that little bitch pay.

Chapter 14

Kevin nudged Jackie. "Mmph. Hon, it's your phone."

Jackie fumbled for her cell on the nightstand and opened one eye in the dimly lit room; the sun had just risen. She grabbed the ringing cell and checked the time: Saturday morning, five after seven. Normally Jackie was up and exercising or on her way to the office during the week. But she and Kevin were in a fit of passion, meaning she could stay the night without regret. Kevin even made a comment at two o'clock that she was obviously not leaving anytime soon as, at that precise moment, Jackie was on her knees grabbing the headboard as Kevin knelt behind her and devoured the nape of her neck. Plus, Kevin made spectacular breakfast, so the decision to stay was a no-brainer.

"Um, hello? Jackie Dekker."

"Ms. Dekker, this is Agent Farris, sorry to call so early, did I wake you?"

Jackie sat up and immediately sprung to life. "No, not at all. I was just, ah, what can I do for you?"

"Ms. Dekker, I reached out last night to Gary Maxwell. He is cuffed to a hospital bed at Northwestern Memorial recovering from last week fracas. He was a little out of it but he made it clear he wouldn't talk to me unless you were there too. Considering his fragile health, I really need you to come to Chicago this morning to escort me to his room. I need him to open up and he apparently won't do it without you."

Jackie cleared the cobwebs out of her head and focused. "Yes, absolutely. I can be there in a few hours."

Kevin heard Jackie's comment and sat up, wiping his eyes.

"No Ms. Dekker, let's call it noon. Give you a chance to wake up.

Meet me in the waiting room at the hospital and we'll go up together."

Jackie assured him she'd be there and hung up. It would be about a three-hour drive from Springfield to downtown Chicago; she had better shower.

"Kevin, I have to meet that inspector at the hospital, Mr. Maxwell won't talk with me there."

"He really seems to like you, the old guy. Then again, you're the only one that thinks he's innocent."

"I feel guilty I haven't seen him since this all went down, he's been there over a week, cut off from everything. And I couldn't even visit. Boss' orders." Jackie threw off the blankets and opened the blinds. The sun streamed through the window, illuminating her naked figure in the morning light.

Kevin made a low growl. "Mm, come back to bed. We have a little time."

"Can't, I have to shower. And you have to make me something to eat before I go."

Jackie hopped in the shower while the aroma of maple and bacon wafted through the apartment. At first, she had taken to keeping a nightshirt and toothbrush at his place. Then an extra pair of panties and some makeup only made sense. And what's another pair of jeans and a few more shoes? Soon, she commandeered an entire dresser drawer and part of his bathroom vanity.

By the time she dried her hair and got dressed, a grand breakfast of French toast, bacon, juice, and coffee awaited her. In spite of her rush to get out the door, she paused for a leisurely meal and traded sections of the paper with Kevin. If she didn't know any better, she might've thought she was falling in love with him, though she'd resisted saying it the night before in the throes of several bed-shaking orgasms.

They finished up and she grabbed her briefcase. Kevin stole a kiss and told her he loved her; Jackie laughed and said, "Aww, you're sweet. I think you are just super." They laughed and he playfully tickled her in an effort to extract what he wanted to hear. But she was having too much fun to surrender.

She kissed him again, grabbed her coat and headed out for Chicago.

The miles ticked by and the farms turned to homes, which turned to industrial parks, then freight trains and semis; Chicago was up ahead. She hadn't been back since it all ended, and she felt as if she were heading into the belly of the beast. For all of its charm that drew Jackie there as a young intern and then a full-fledged prosecutor, deep down she was convinced the city consumed souls. It took Tina Haise, Gary Maxwell, and of course Joe Haise. The longer they stayed, the darker they became. Even her colleague, now federal judge, Nate Washington made cryptic remarks about how evil it all was and how Joe Haise devoured his humanity. But the action, the restaurants, theaters, and nightclubs were unmatched. Anxiety crept into her gut as she passed Midway Airport on the Stevenson and entered city limits. She loved and hated this place.

Chapter 15

Horace was going to need money. Not a lot, but enough to start up in Illinois. He learned Springfield was not far from Chicago. He read that Chicago had gangsters, which sounded cool, but Springfield was smaller and quiet. He would indeed be a big fish in a small pond. Paying for airfare was easy; he occasionally would take out a credit card in Noah's name and keep it for emergencies. Noah had a number of creditors after him at any given time, though he was uncollectable and they usually just let him be. Horace still had two credit cards for Noah he never used, surely one of them still worked.

He spent a few weeks squirreling away funds, a few dollars here and there, an unattended purse was always good and he managed a few stolen bikes that he then offered on a street corner for fifty bucks each. By the weekend, he had two grand in his pocket and a plane ticket to Springfield. That's when he bumped into Reverend Jeremiah.

Jeremiah was a six-foot five, skinny white street hustler, Horace always considered himself a cut above. But they had mutual respect for one another, if not admiration, as their marks rarely overlapped. Jeremiah ran three-card Monte, sold a little marijuana, and was known as the best short-change artist in the western hemisphere, while Horace wore a button-down shirt and leased office space for his scams.

They bumped into each other in a parking lot when Horace was walking out with a new carry-on suitcase.

Jeremiah approached him and spoke first. "Sir, do you have two tens for a twenty? My daughter needs...oh, didn't see you there, Horace. Thought you were a tourist."

The two shook hands and completed an awkward bro-hug. "Reverend. How's business?"

"Slow, keep thinking the Islands are about tapped out for me. Looks like you goin' on a trip." He pointed to Horace's purchase.

"Maybe. Gonna try the mainland for a spell. Keep it on the D-L, need to get away quiet."

"No worries, women after you again?"

"Nah, it's just goin' dry for me too. Need a change of scenery, try something new. Maybe Chicago."

"You goin' to Chicago? Want to make some extra? I could use some help with Chicago and the money's quick."

Horace eyed him warily. Though the Reverend was reliable, they always avoided doing business together, lest they spend time trying to hustle each other when there were better pigeons out there.

"I'm not hauling weed through an airport. Dogs now, you know."

"Nah, Horace, better than weed. Snakes."

Horace cocked his head. "Snakes? You mean, dicks? I ain't sucking dick in Chicago. I don't need money that bad."

"No, man. Real snakes. Virgin Islands Tree Boa, man. They are really hard to get in Chicago and I got a guy offering me three grand a pop. I'll split half with you for every one you can bring to my guys up there."

"Why can't you just mail them? Or have him come get a few?"

"Nah, man. Vaccination records, quarantine fees; it ain't worth it. Look, they're really small and harmless. I'll give you a bunch in a pillowcase. Just throw it in the fridge for an hour, they get cold and fall asleep. Toss the bag in your luggage, my buddy here will run it past security. There is no customs because we are the US, so no cops. You get off the flight and my guy in Chicago will hand you an envelope and take the bag off the carousel. Boom. He'll send me my cut. No worries."

"Fifteen hundred per?"

"Solid. My cousin can gather them tonight. Prolly get ten or so. Fifteen grand in your pocket."

The expression on Horace's face betrayed his cool attitude. The Reverend had him.

"Fine, but you put them in your fridge. Gimme the bag tomorrow and tell your guy I will be at the airport at one o'clock for my flight at two.

So he needs to be ready."

"Yeah, no worries. Done." The two men exchanged details and the Reverend promised to deliver the bag at a quarter to one. Horace had to time it just right.

The next day, Horace carefully packed his luggage. He had little to take, and if Stella stopped by his place and saw things missing, she'd get suspicious. But a carry-on held all of Horace's worldly possessions. He placed it in the trunk of his rusted Buick and drove to the office as if nothing were out of sorts. The plan was to fly to Chicago direct, take a Greyhound to Springfield, and make his way from there. With fifteen to twenty grand in his pocket, he wouldn't even need his latest sucker Louisa to make a go of it.

He arrived at the office as usual; Stella was already there and making flirtatious small talk. Horace tried to appear casual, though he was distracted by the clock. Almost noon Noah rolled in, took a seat, and fell asleep. Horace kept checking the clock, his nervous excitement was rushing through his body. The high was better than any scam he ran, he was leaving, maybe forever. He wiped his palms on his pants and tried to calm his mind.

"Well, I think I am going to grab a bite." He stood, cracked his knuckles, and sauntered toward the door. "I may make a stop before I get back, need to see someone to get paid from an old thing."

Uncle Noah grunted, Stella continued to file her nails and muttered a goodbye. Horace walked out of the office. Unable to control himself, he sprinted to his car. He was like a prisoner being given the keys to the gate, he couldn't remember ever feeling a thrill like this.

He peeled out of the lot and sped away, leaving his life in the rearview mirror. Five minutes later, he pulled over at an intersection. A lanky white man emerged with a black gym bag, nearly bursting at the seams. He leaned in the passenger window and smiled at Horace.

"Here it is, they were in the fridge so they sleepin' now. There are twenty in there, my cousin did great." He withdrew his head and dropped the fat bag on the seat. Jeremiah unzipped the bag, revealing a bulging white pillowcase. The telltale outline of twenty snakes made Horace smile; to anyone else, it looked like a bundle of snakes. To Horace, it was money.

Thirty grand, in all.

"One problem. My guy in Chicago got arrested on some parking tickets. Take the bag with you and he'll meet you tomorrow to get it."

"Tomorrow? I'm going to be in Springfield tonight. I can't drive back to Chicago tomorrow. I don't even know where to go in Chicago. He is supposed to be at the airport, you asshole!"

"Relax, man. My guy will drive to you, it is worth it. Just keep the snakes tonight. They don't need food, just give them some air. I'll throw in an extra hundred per snake, okay? I'll call you tomorrow, tell me the address where you'll be in Springton and he'll find you."

"Spring*field*, goddamn it. This is so fucking bad."

"Relax, Horace. Wanna hit before you go? I got some good shit here." Jeremiah began fishing in his pocket.

"No, for chrissakes. I hate fucking snakes."

"You fuck snakes?" Reverend began chuckling.

"Nah, I mean I fucking hate snakes."

"It's all good, man. Now at the airport here in town, my guy is Louis. He looks like me. Tall, skinny, white guy. He is looking for you. He'll meet you at the ticket counter. Good luck, see you when you whenever."

They shook, Horace patted the gym bag, and pulled into traffic. He looked back and saw Jeremiah wave, the only goodbye he got. He couldn't keep his eye off his prize, Horace loathed snakes but loved money. Twenty minutes later, he pulled into the parking garage at the airport, removed his carry-on and the black bag, and shut the car door. He reared back and heaved his keys as far as he could. "Good riddance," he muttered quietly and walked across the lot to the door to the departure gates. He entered and, seeing no one like the Reverend, he proceeded to a kiosk and printed his boarding pass. He approached a ticket agent and almost immediately spotted a lanky nervous-looking baggage handler behind the ticket counter. Horace caught his eye and nodded, he nodded back. *It's on.*

Horace approached and offered a muted greeting to an indifferent woman in a blue blazer. "Boarding pass?"

Horace handed it over as the lanky kid tried to casually pace behind the counter, shuttling between agents and scooping bags off the scale. As Horace placed the snakes on the scale, the agent barely looked up as she typed. A printer spit out the luggage receipt, the baggage handler immediately tore it off the machine. "I can help with this, Mona." She never looked up from her screen as the boy and the bag disappeared into the back.

Easier than I thought. Horace breathed a sigh of relief and practically sprinted to the gate. He was distracted the entire flight. Staring out the window, calculating his cut from the snakes, planning his next moves. *Maybe I'll get in with a gang like Capone, wear nice suits and everything.* He was like a kid on his way to Disney World.

Six hours later, Horace landed and nervously hustled to the carousel to retrieve the snakes. Constantly looking over his shoulder for Customs Agents, he only saw tired travelers and indifferent airport staff. As if on cue, his bag was the first on the carousel. Horace waited to approach the bag until he was certain no one was conducting surveillance. Casually, he snatched it up and headed for the door. As he approached the sliding glass doors that stood between him and freedom, he felt a hand on his shoulder and turned to see a Cook County Sheriff. Horace nearly soiled himself.

"Buddy, you left your carry-on back there." He pointed back to the carousel where Horace' suitcase stood.

Horace forced a laugh. "Oh, thanks, man. These flights make me crazy." The deputy walked off and Horace grabbed his case and sprinted out the door, committing himself to a life of charity and piety as the Lord clearly bailed his ass out of a jam. He made it to the Greyhound desk and onto the Springfield bus. He couldn't believe his luck.

It wouldn't last.

As the bus pulled into the main Springfield depot, an odor began to permeate through the cabin. A mixture of road kill and ammonia, passengers began looking around their seats for the offender as the acrid odor grew stronger. After shutting off the engine, the driver bolted out the doors, followed by passengers holding their noses. The group stood outside as the luggage hatches opened, throwing a blast of foul odor at them. One elderly woman vomited as gracefully as possible in a trash can. The driver held his nose and threw luggage out until a gray-white liquid was seen oozing from a bag. Horace' bag. The driver saw the name and pointed at Horace; other drivers, seeing the commotion, ran over and surrounded him, yelling for him to stay put.

Unbeknownst to Horace, Virgin Islands Tree Boas, like many other snakes, vomit when nervous or threatened. The Reverend Jeremiah fed the snakes immediately before the flight, assuming they would sleep after a meal. Instead, they woke from their slumber in the luggage hold of the bus and collectively horked half-digested mice all over one another. Fearing the odor related to a portable crystal meth lab—not his first encounter with one—the driver called 911. Horace was placed in the back of a squad car until the Springfield police could figure out what the hell to do with him. Between the US Virgin Islands boarding pass in his pants and his lack of a decent cover story, it wasn't long before the cops figured where the snakes came from. Horace learned what the Reverend failed to disclose: the reason people were willing to pay so much for a single Tree Boa is because they are endangered and the importation of them is a federal offense. Cops from three different agencies hauled him off to jail for violation of the Lacey Act, which bans the transportation of endangered species across state or international lines and is punishable by up to five years in prison and a $250,000 fine.

Horace suddenly missed the Islands.

Chapter 16

Joe spent Saturday morning singing, "We Built This City" by Starship in the shower and shaving his body smooth. After nearly an hour, he emerged from the cloud of steam looking like a hairless wrinkled middle-aged porn star. More time spent in front of the vanity whistling, "How Can we Be Lovers" by Michael Bolton, combing and re-combing his hair and shaving his face. He finished off with a generous coating of baby oil, giving him a slick sheen. He winked at himself in the mirror and headed to the bedroom singing, "Sussudio" by Phil Collins. He selected a worn pair of thrift store jeans and a rough sweatshirt from a college he never heard of and a dark tan jacket with holes in the sleeves. He donned a pair of thick socks and heavy workboots to handle the Chicago winter, and finished off his look with a green John Deere ballcap and dark gray scarf. He returned to the bathroom mirror to admire himself.

Yes. Yes, yes, yes. Look at this. Boom. Are you afraid, my little morsel? Mm, you should be.

Joe popped his jacket collar, adjusted the scarf, and pulled down the brim of his cap, completely concealing his face. He smiled and shut out the light. He stopped by the den and fired up the computer. After accessing his usual security protocols, he sent a single message.

Leaving in a few hours, Uber will pick you up you at 9:00 and we'll meet there!

He logged off and returned to the dining room and stripped naked, laying each item of clothing on the table. He removed a roll of packing tape from a bureau drawer and pulled out a three-foot strip. Starting with the boots, he began meticulously applying the tape to one side of the shoe, patting it firmly on the leather, then slowly pulled the tape off, removing every particle of matter. He started to sing, "More Than A Feeling" by

Boston as he peeled off another strip of tape, flipped the boot, and began the process again. This would be a long, tedious day, but a very busy night.

***

Jackie checked the GPS on her phone several times until she could see Northwestern Memorial Hospital in the distance. She found the Huron Street parking entrance, took a ticket, and found a spot. She hadn't seen Gary Maxwell since the courtroom melee and realized she was excited to see her friend.

Friend? Is he a friend? What else would he be to me? Stepfather?

Jackie was almost a half-hour early. *Maybe Farris is already in his room. Will there be a police guard outside the door like in the movies?* She followed the signs to the receptionist and signed in. Like all visitors, she forgot half the directions they gave her, wandered around the hospital for ten minutes, and finally gave up and asked a nurse for help.

"Room 3225 dear, at the end of the hall on the left."

Jackie walked down the hall, unconsciously slowing her pace as she approached the door. She saw the name scrawled on the plate next to the door, "Maxwell, G."

She knocked softly and eased the door open.

"Hello? Mr. Maxwell?"

The scent of disinfectant hung in the air, she peered in to see a small figure drowning in blankets. The room was dim, lit only by the various monitors quietly beeping and pulsing next to the bed. He didn't move.

She moved closer and he came into view. The man she knew from visits to Menard Correctional was gone. The charming, but slightly ill, financial wizard was now a cancer-riddled shell of a man. She could barely breathe.

The figure coughed, stirred a bit, and opened his eyes. He turned his head and looked at her with an expression of confusion, then broke into a smile. A raspy voice spoke to her.

"Ms. Dekker? Oh, my dear. I was hoping you'd stop by." He reached for a control pad and pressed a button, causing the head of his bed to rise. Soon he was sitting up, smiling warmly at his guest.

Jackie smiled back walked over to him. "Mr. Maxwell, so good to see you someplace other than court or prison." She leaned in and placed a gentle kiss on his forehead. He reached up to hug her, but one hand rattled at his side; he lay cuffed to the bed.

She pulled up a chair and sat next to the man she once loathed as a murderer, then respected as a complicated but brilliant witness, then embraced as a lonely, innocent man.

"I don't have many visitors, as usual. My ex-wife Veronica is still at our vacation property in Marseilles with the girls. I told her not to come back, just too dangerous. Honestly, I still have resources and could arrange for her security overseas, but I don't want the girls to see me like this. Best they remember me as a strong father who had some trouble with the law."

Jackie's heart nearly broke. Maxwell had twin daughters that fled the country in fear with their mother after someone—Joe Haise, no doubt—attacked her and put the fear of God in her. Surely, he did it to keep Maxwell from accusing Joe on the stand, which he'd done anyway.

"Mr. Maxwell, I won't rest until your daughters know their father was an innocent man."

He smiled. "Good girl. Because I won't ever leave this place, of that the doctors are certain. But you take care, dear. Haise is a bastard. Killed his wife, framed me, and rolled in his own stink the whole time. He won't hesitate to harm you."

"No worries, I was transferred down south and I have a bodyguard at work that played one year for the Bears. I'll be just fine."

"Thank the Lord for that one. And what about our secret?" He was referring to the fact the Tina Haise was an escort.

"No one knows but you, me, and *him*." Jackie emphasized the last word with a hiss.

"Good enough. Respect her memory, least we can do."

"Mr. Maxwell, a Federal Agent from the Inspector General is coming here any minute. He said you wouldn't talk to him without me."

He endeavored to speak though he suffered labored breathing. "Oh, that. I wanted to see you and I thought if I told him I needed you here, he'd make that happen. I'll take care of him, dear. Just hold my hand for a minute."

Jackie smiled. Maxwell always worked an angle, even on his deathbed. She dutifully held his hand as a loud knock startled her and the door creaked open.

"Mr. Maxwell? It's Agent Farris."

***

Joe parked his car and carefully moved the stack of old, worn clothing from the passenger seat to the floor in the back, on top of the boots. He climbed out of the car and strolled into The Citadel lobby. Joe walked confidently to the coat check girl, removed his topcoat and handed it over.

"Well, aren't you a lovely warm thing on a cold night!" Joe smiled and raised his eyebrows.

A young brunette smiled and took Joe's coat, pulled a tag off a hanger and handed it to Joe.

"Lucky number twenty-one! Did you know that Cleopatra was twenty-one when Caesar took her as his lover? He was fifty-two. Isn't that romantic? An older man and a younger woman. I bet you're twenty-one, am I right?"

The young girl turned beet red, and became visibly uncomfortable. "Well, I'm not supposed to talk to the theater-goers about things like that. My manager said—"

"No worries, my dear Cleopatra. See you in two hours!"

Joe bounded off to the ticket taker, the same woman working the previous night. He produced the ticket he printed out at home with a cheery smile. "Evening my dear! Ready for a night of great experimental theater?"

The woman smiled and took his paper. "Well, I certainly am! You just head right down the hall and through those doors on the right."

Joe took his receipt and began to walk through as she paused before releasing the stub from her grip.

"Were you here once before?"

Joe froze and swallowed hard. "'Fraid not, first time actually."

She looked embarrassed. "Oh, well I must be mistaken. Enjoy your evening."

Joe smiled and continued on. As the small crowd began moving toward the theater doors, Joe made a beeline for the restroom. When he was certain no one was looking, he slipped out a side door and casually strolled back to his car. He climbed in, started the engine, and eased his way out of the parking lot. He drove for several minutes, then pulled off into the parking lot of an office building and awkwardly changed clothes in the front seat. He concluded by wrapping himself with the scarf and pulled the ball cap down tightly on his head. He then patiently spent a full five minutes adjusting the radio and searching for a station with some killer 80's music. When Huey Lewis and The News blared through the speakers, Joe cranked the volume and slipped out of the parking lot and into traffic.

He drove a circuitous route, exiting the expressway and reentering, doubling back, and pausing at a yellow light only to accelerate through the moment the light turned red. He executed U-turns, Y-turns, and doubled back over his route twice. Certain that no one could have seen him, followed him, tracked him, or remembered his car, he headed to his target. It had been a hell of a week finally he was going to have some fun.

He checked his watch, 8:55. It's time to go. He drove several blocks and pulled over to park on the shoulder. The street was located in the heart of Wicker Park, a neighborhood that Forbes Magazine called "The Midwest Mecca of Hipsterdom." It is a gritty enclave of tattoo artists and alt-rock band enthusiasts, the perfect place to be, for one particular person anyway. He waited patiently, gripping the wheel though thick ski gloves, staring at the empty stoop of a brownstone a half block ahead. Joe turned off the radio; he needed to focus. 9:02.

He drummed his fingers on the wheel, slowed his breathing, and waited. He would not display the lack of discipline he had in the past. He would be in total control. 9:05. Finally, a slight figure emerged and lit a cigarette.

Aww, hi baby. Your watch broke?

Joe puckered his lips and offered a distant kiss. *Mwah.*

When the figure threw the cigarette on the ground and crushed it out, Joe adjusted his cap, scarf, and popped the collar of his coat. He turned on the headlights, pulled away from the curb, and drove down the street. He saw his prey looking lost, but then offering a sweet smile as the car pulled up to the curb in front of the brownstone. Joe lowered the window as the figure approached the car and leaned in the window.

"Hiya, are you the Uber driver?"

Joe muffled his response with a slightly altered voice through a thick scarf.

"Sure am, are you Jammer Franks?"

**

Agent Farris sat next to the hospital bed on the far side. He appeared to take notice that Jackie was sitting opposite holding Maxwell's frail hand, but he said nothing.

"Now Mr. Maxwell, let's get to it. As I explained the last time I was here, you made some very strong allegations in court against Joseph Haise, a respected federal prosecutor."

"I did no such thing. I made an accusation against a narcissistic sociopath. Big difference."

Agent Farris came dangerously close to a chuckle, but stopped short. "Very well. You asked for Ms. Dekker to be present when we spoke. Why did you do that?"

Farris noted Maxwell seemed to get stronger by the minute. "I haven't seen but one pretty face in years. And I've found my memory improves when I'm in the company of a charming woman. Don't you, Agent Farris?"

Jackie noticed Farris reached a finger up and scratched the corner of his mouth. *Is he concealing a smile?*

"Very well, I'll be quick. I know you tend to tire easily. Mr. Maxwell, did you, at any time, indicate to Ms. Dekker that you were going to make that accusation in open court?"

"Heavens, no. If I had, she never would have put me on the stand in that federal courtroom. You think I wanted to jeopardize that? If I did such a thing, I would have rotted in that tomb over the river from"—He paused for dramatic effect—"St. Louis. That's in Missouri, of all places."

Farris and Jackie both coughed to mask something approaching a laugh.

Farris collected himself. "I see. Now, Mr. Maxwell, I must ask why you said that on the stand. If you lied, you will be charged with perjury. Maybe you think it doesn't matter at this point. But I will personally see to it you are removed from this medical Four Seasons and we'll take you back to the Howard Johnson's that is the Menard Correctional Infirmary."

Maxwell's smile vanished and he appeared to shrink in his bed. "Agent Farris, I will only say this once. I know that I had an intimate evening with the late Mrs. Haise on that fateful night years ago. I will tell you she left my house in perfect health. I will tell you I heard a ruckus and ran down to the driveway in my bathrobe to find Mrs. Haise dead. I bent down to render aid, but she was gone, so I just held her. That's when the paperboy drove up, saw me, and jumped out with his cellphone in hand. I panicked and ran inside to call my attorney. The police arrested me when I was on the phone with him, as a matter of fact."

"Naturally, the real killer conveniently appeared in the exact moment after she walked out, but before the paperboy arrived." Farris scribbled furiously and tried to sound skeptical. Jackie couldn't quite tell, but began to suspect he was putting on an act.

"Agent Farris, I will be dead before the next oil change on your car is due. Do you honestly think I care if you believe me?"

"Fair point. So why do you think Joe Haise was that mysterious stranger in your driveway?"

Maxwell showed a flash of a smile. "I took my measure of the man after she died. Agent Farris, I can size a man up in a minute. I dare say I am one of the best of the world at it. I could buy and sell everyone you know. Well, before my wife, her lawyers, and your boy Haise took a piece of my fortune, that is. Reading people is what I do. For instance, I know you are whip-smart and loathe Haise as much as we both do." He squeezed Jackie's hand reassuringly. "I saw Haise in court every time I had a hearing. I read his bullshit interviews in the paper. I saw his phony manufactured grief. He killed her. And everyone in this room knows it."

Farris stopped writing and locked his gaze with Jackie. For the first time, she met his stare and didn't flinch. Maxwell was right, he saw right through Haise and now Farris, and for the first time, Farris had no follow-up questions or retorts. He put away his notebook and shut off his recorder. Farris became human for an instant. "We have nothing on Haise. You have nothing on Haise. And unless I find a miracle in the next week, he's gonna skate on the murder of Tina Haise."

Maxwell added, "Or Ms. Dekker's worst first date in the world, that Todd Perry fellow."

Farris nodded somberly and leveled his gaze at Maxwell. "Yep, him too. Right now, all I have on him is a weak stalking charge against young Ms. Dekker here, which unless I can rattle him, won't connect to the murder of Tina Haise. The GPS under her car traced back to a spy store in Kenosha. Detective Buddy Scott from Winnetka PD went to that store and found a hangaround kid who will claim Haise purchased a similar unit a few months earlier and spoke to him for ten minutes about the specs. We know he bought it for Tina Haise' car, but can't prove it because it wasn't there by the time the cops got to your house. We also know the exact same type of GPS was found under Ms. Dekker's car, but we have no eyewitness to prove he bought that one. Basically, we have half a case of everything, which is useless. But I am going to ask that a grand jury be convened ASAP so that I can take your sworn statement by video as soon as possible. I need to preserve your testimony because, as callous as this sounds, you won't be here for the trial." Though the comment hung heavy in the air, they all knew he was right. "Can we get that into trial evidence, Ms. Dekker?"

Jackie exhaled through pursed lips. "Whew, it is all kinds of hearsay and Haise would never get to confront his accuser in court, which is a Sixth Amendment no-no. But if Mr. Maxwell is, um, unavailable for trial, we can try to offer his statement as some kind of corroboration evidence. It is a longshot, but it is better than nothing. And the mere spectacle of it could at least end his career."

They all paused to take in the futility of the situation. Jackie piped up. "See, maybe we can't prove up the high burden of proof for a criminal charge of murder or stalking, but Joe can be fired for cause, which is almost anything. When the spy store kid picks Joe out of a lineup, he'll never again set foot in a federal courtroom."

***

"Jammer, that's an unusual name."

"Yeah, well, fucking Mom was nuts. You know?"

He fidgeted in the back seat. Joe watched him wearily through the rearview mirror. He sported calloused fingertips, sallow cheeks, and he kept jerking involuntarily. Joe knew a meth tweaker when he saw one.

"Oh, my mother was a doozy, pal. Real strong ideas of the Bible and punishment. If I even looked at the lingerie ads in the Penny's catalogue, I'd get a whooping. One time she made me wear her bra and panties for an hour, told me if I wanted to look at 'em, I should have to wear 'em."

The kid was barely able to pay attention. "Fucking parents, man. Fuck. You know where we're going?"

Joe nodded. "Oh yes. Your date for the evening, Stephanie is it? Arranged everything and prepaid my fare. I am to take you to meet her. She sounds lovely."

Jammer suddenly got interested. "Oh yeah, she's fucking smoking. Found me on Facebook. Apparently, she knew someone I know and we met at a party or something. Said I was cute and she was too shy to ask me out back then. Looks like a fucking model. So, I came from Kenosha last night and my buddy let me crash at his place. Going to meet her tonight."

Joe was smiling under his scarf. "Well, I'm sure it will be a night you'll never forget. Or remember."

They drove through the streets and Joe made sure to keep him distracted with conversation as he entered into an industrial park. As the minutes passed, the streets became darker and more desolate, until he turned down a dead-end street. In the heart of Chicago, they were a thousand miles from civilization. Jammer began to look out the windows nervously.

"Yo man, you sure this is it?"

Joe pulled over to the side of the street and shut off the engine. "Yes sir, something about a rave in that warehouse at the end of the road. You are the third fare I've driven here in the last hour. Both were carloads of girls, half naked in this weather, if you can imagine such a thing."

Jammer's face lit up. "Really? Fucking sweet."

"I'll get the door sir, you sit tight."

Jammer seemed to enjoy being pampered, he was happy to recline in a warm car while some guy waited on him. The door opened and he stepped out. Joe pointed down the road.

"The rave is down there; see that door on the side? Way over there?"

As Jammer squinted hard to see the door that the man insisted was there, he didn't notice the driver step behind him. Nor did he notice the driver rear back a heavy winter boot. In an instant, Joe let fly a kick between Jammer's legs, connecting with his groin.

In the moment between the brutal contact and the pain registering in his nerve endings and sending signals to his drug-addled brain, Jammer spun around and faced his driver.

"Hey man, what the h—?"

Before he could finish his sentence, he collapsed in agony. A spilt second after he hit the ground, Joe removed his cap and scarf and landed on top of his victim, using his knees to pin Jammer's frail arms to the ground as he wrapped his hands around the kid's throat. A moment before he passed out, Jammer recognized the face of the last person he would ever see. As he began to fade into oblivion, his brain tried to form the words, "You're that guy…" But no sound accompanied the movement of his lips. He blacked out in moments.

Joe continued to apply pressure for several minutes, until he was certain. Joe quickly re-wrapped the scarf and pulled the cap on tight. He stood and looked around to confirm no one saw his charitable act of ridding the world of a complete waste of valuable carbon. He very carefully grabbed the kid's jacket, dragged him into an alley, and propped him against a wall under some garbage bags. With any luck, he'd be taken for a hobo and ignored for several days. Joe stripped off his own clothes and tossed them on the passenger seat as he put on his theater clothes once again. He ran back to the car and very casually drove away, tossing the worn clothes out the window, item by item, every mile he drove. He sped back to the theater and paused at the parking lot entrance. 9:55. The eight o'clock show would be letting out in moments. Joe found a parking spot in the back and shut off the engine. He walked up to the doors and peered in. The lobby was empty. The ticket-taker was gone. Joe checked his watch and waited. He wasn't cold; we wasn't even impatient. He simply waited.

Minutes later, he heard what could only be the crescendo of the awful closing number, followed by a smattering of polite but pitiable applause that would not be out of place at a golf tournament after someone putted out for a double bogey. He put his head down, opened the doors, and slipped into the lobby as the first patrons exited from the theater. No one noticed the man waiting in the corner, he was simply a theatergoer who had the good sense to leave this abortion of a theater production in time to avoid the grand finale number, "Mucus Plug Mambo." Poor bastards, Joe thought.

As the men began lining up at the coat check, Joe slipped in line and made an attempt at small talk with the other patrons, grumbling about the waste of time that was their Saturday night. Joe made it to the counter and produced his ticket.

"Hello, my Cleopatra!"

The young girl forced a smile and retrieved Joe's coat. He took it and in made a showing of removing a twenty-dollar bill from his pocket and placed it in the tip basket.

"That's for you, Your Highness. Queen of all of Egypt!" She smiled genuinely and Joe made for the door. He headed out into the cold Chicago night with a spring in his step. He climbed in his car, turned on the radio, and fiddled with the knob until he discovered "Far From Over" by Frank Stallone. Joe yelled, "Fuck yes!" and sang as loud as he could the entire way home.

Chapter 17

Joe Haise was right; it took three days before someone discovered the body of Jammer Franks. His eyes bulged out of his head and his face frozen in an expression of shock. It took hours before anyone was able to put two and two together and contacted the US Attorney for the Northern District of Illinois, The Honorable Dave Dunham. When he learned his only witness to any malfeasance by his suspended White Collar Fraud Section Chief was murdered in a rundown industrial park, the shit hit the fan. The DOJ Inspector General hopped a plane from DC to Chicago. A US Marshal waited at O'Hare to drive him straight to the Dirksen Federal Building as soon as he landed. Agent Farris, because of his ability to rattle Joe Haise, was to conduct an interrogation once they had enough to bring him in for questioning.

The original investigator on the Tina Haise murder, Winnetka Detective Buddy Scott, cut short a vacation to return home. He was more than eager to assist, expressing his fervent desire to right a wrong and vowed that Joe Haise wasn't going to get away with it again. He volunteered to spend the day with the coroner and the Chicago PD evidence techs to see what they could find that might tie Joe to the murder.

Jackie Dekker was spending a slow Wednesday in the office working on a paper she hoped to submit to the Illinois Bar Journal on a proposed change to the federal sentencing guidelines for market manipulation offenses, when she looked up to see Roz Jeffries standing in her doorway.

"Roz! Hey, come on in. Let me move some of these files." Roz closed the door, shooed Jackie back to her chair, and cleared off a seat. Jackie noted she wasn't smiling.

"Jackie, we need to talk."

Jackie listened as Roz spoke. Her mouth went dry and her stomach turned knots. She began to shake. By the time Roz finished, a tear ran down Jackie's cheek. She spoke for the first time through a weak, defeated voice.

"He's going to freaking kill me."

"Not in a million years! Nothing is going to happen to happen to you. We upped security around here and he is going to be brought in for questioning back in Chicago."

"They are wasting their time. He won't confess and they won't find anything. He's too fucking smart."

Roz nodded somberly. "You may be right. I told you I met him once, didn't I?"

"You said you never did like him on my first day here."

"Six or seven years ago I was working in Chicago. They brought me in as Special Counsel on a case because they had a conflict and they wanted me to help out. The case involved a former DEA evidence tech named Vicki Marvin that stole weapons and drugs from the lockup on cases that were sent to the archives. She sold the stuff and pocketed the money. She got away with it for years before a cold case squad looking into a possible wrongful conviction called back an old box and discovered the gun missing and the drugs cut down to nothing. They suspected her immediately and nailed her in a sting. She tried to hide the money in a few different accounts and I needed to tie her to the proceeds, so I asked for assistance from the White Collar section and guess who they gave me."

"Our best buddy."

"Bingo. He was happily married back then and I had no idea anything was amiss. I showed him what I found and asked for some help. He reviewed my memos and reports and began marking them up, grading them like a high school English teacher. He actually wrote in the margin of an internal memo that I used a split infinitive. When I saw his changes, I stormed into his office and asked what the hell he was doing, that I didn't need English composition help, I needed to trace the money to Vicki. He looked at me and said, 'One little mistake like this, dear Rosalyn, is how empires are brought down.' He sat back with a shit-eating grin and waited for me to thank him. I left and vowed never to talk to him again. He's an asshole of Olympic proportions. Fuck him and the horse he rode in on."

Jackie began frantically gathering her things. "Roz, I need to see Judge Washington in Peoria. He's a friend from Chicago and he'll know what to do. I need to see him today."

"Take a car from the motor pool and get out of here. But one of the guys is going to follow you out of the city and they'll make sure someone is waiting for you when you get to the courthouse in Peoria."

"Ok, thanks Roz. Honestly, I don't know how I can ever repay you for all you've done for me. If you need me to work extra, even if it isn't fraud, just do whatever, then I'm your girl."

Roz displayed a delightfully evil grin. "Now that you mention it, what do you know about the Virgin Islands Tree Boa?"

"I'm sorry, the *what*, now?"

"It can wait until you return. Get going."

Jackie grabbed her purse and coat and bolted for the door, snatching a set of keys from Ruth. Jackie found the blue Crown Victoria in the lot; her heart was racing as she climbed in and squealed out of the parking garage. She didn't know that Roz was already on the phone to the Honorable Nate Washington about the visitor he could expect in an hour.

Her phoned beeped as she drove, she saw an incoming text from Kevin. *Not today, can't do this today. Not today.* She tossed the phone on the passenger seat and pressed on the gas. An hour later, she arrived at the federal courthouse. It was a formal gray stone structure, but not quite as imposing as Springfield. She parked and found the main entrance. Before she could open the door, it opened for her and a US Marshal stepped out.

"Ms. Dekker? Judge Washington is waiting for you."

She followed him in and they bypassed the security checkpoint, heading straight down a hall, through a locked door, and to a large wooden office door adorned with a sign that read, *Chambers of the Honorable Nathan Washington*. The Marshal knocked once and opened the door.

"Jackie? Where is the fair maiden, Jacqueline?"

Jackie walked in and smiled. "My handsome squire, it has been too long."

Washington waved away the marshal, who closed the door behind him. Nate's massive frame walked toward her with his arms outstretched.

Jackie ran to him and they embraced. Jackie felt truly safe in his grasp and her body shuddered as she began to cry.

"Now, now, my turtledove. You are safe in my castle."

She laughed through the tears and held him a moment longer.

They spent an hour catching up. Jackie barely saw her old colleague since he'd been appointed to the bench. Only Nate could understand her predicament.

"Jackie, you're right. Joe wouldn't have done this on a lark; he is always two steps ahead. But you aren't going back to Chicago; Springfield is going to be your permanent assignment. Roz Jeffries and I fixed it."

She closed her eyes and exhaled. "Thank God, Nate. I think I really like it here."

"Are you still seeing that bike path engineer? We should have dinner sometime. Ernest found a job here so we can hang out."

"Kevin, yeah. I'm still seeing him. Honestly Nate, so much is going on I can't even think about him right now."

"Don't let Joe Haise run your life from 200 miles away. Don't give him the satisfaction."

"I won't, Nate. Can I ask a question? You said once that Joe had dibs on your soul. What did you mean? Why do you think you owe him something?"

Nate said nothing. He stood and ran his hands over his bald head and walked to his desk. He poured two small tumblers of scotch and wordlessly handed one to Jackie. He tipped his glass to her and took a healthy gulp. She paused, contemplating an answer, and swallowed hard.

"It's not important right now. Listen, keep your head down and let Dave Dunham and the gang do their thing. They'll burn his ass and you are so far down the list of people he doesn't like. Live your life, they'll get him. Someone will get him, I guarantee it."

Jackie swallowed the entire contents of her glass and coughed. Her eyes watered as she exhaled. "Thanks, Nate. You are still my only friend."

"Good girl. Now go home and forget about this madness."

"I will Nate; I just have something to do first."

They hugged one final time and Jackie promised to arrange a dinner in a few weeks when their schedules synched up. Nate walked her to the door to find the marshal waiting in the hallway. He picked up where he left off, walking Jackie to her car. She thanked him and he wished her safe travels back to Springfield. But she was going the other way. She needed to see someone first.

Chapter 18

Joe was dressed and ready when they came for him. He sat formally on a faux Victorian wingback chair engrossed in a crisp copy of Little Women. He noticed faces in the windows a split second before the doorbell rang. He carefully dog-eared the page as he rose, walked to the front door, and opened it with a welcoming smile.

"Agent Farris, well, what I can do for you?"

Farris stood ramrod straight, flanked by four plainclothes and two uniformed officers. He leered at Joe, clearly hoping for a confrontation that would allow him to legally pummel his suspect. Joe would not give him the satisfaction.

"Joe, we need to have a word. Now."

"What about? Is there something wrong?" Joe donned a puzzled expression that took a half hour in the vanity mirror to perfect.

"Can't say right here. We really need to talk someplace more private."

Joe opened the door wide and stepped aside in a grand gesture. "Certainly, come on in gentlemen and I'll put on some tea."

Farris didn't budge. "Think we better do this downtown, Mr. Haise."

If they had a warrant, I'd be in cuffs right now. "Well, as a lawyer, I suppose I could ask if I have a choice. But you've piqued my interest, Agent Farris. I'll grab my coat."

Farris forced his way in. "Let my assistant here get that coat for you. Can't take the chance you have a weapon, now can I?"

Joe acted as if he was a guest of a wonderful host and was sure to be effusive in his praise for their hospitality the entire drive. Farris nearly had steam shooting out of his ears as Haise grated on his nerves. Twenty minutes later, they arrived at the sallyport, an underground garage drop-off at the Dirksen Federal Courthouse.

"Agent Farris, I don't think I'm supposed to be here for another two weeks. I don't want to get into trouble, you know."

Farris did not engage Joe's banter; he exited the car, opened Joe's door, and helped him out. The group of officers filed into the building and into the elevator. As they wordlessly rode up, Joe noted the badges clipped to their coats indicated two were FBI, two were Chicago PD, and his newest best-est buddy Farris was from the Department of Justice.

They exited the elevator in silence and walked down the hallway. Unlike the elegant trappings of the courtroom side of the operations, this floor was linoleum, the lights were bright fluorescent, and the doors to the various rooms were large, heavy, and metal.

They turned a corner and walked to a small room, the door was open and Joe could see a small metal table, two chairs, and a not-too-subtle CCTV camera in a corner of the ceiling. Joe had seen this room dozens of times, but he never sat in the hot seat.

"Shall I sit over there, Agent Farris?" *Let the games begin, you ignorant bastard.*

Farris pointed as he closed the door and the two removed their coats, placed them on the table, and sat opposite each other. The other officers remained outside. Farris unzipped a leather folder and slid a form to Joe.

"Mr. Haise, this says that you are not under arrest, that you are…"

"…free to leave at any time, that I may have a lawyer present, that I agree to talk to you. Really Agent Farris, I've forgotten more about this form than could ever know." Joe reached across the table with an empty hand and wiggled his fingers as he continued to silently read the page. Farris wordlessly placed a pen in Joe's outstretched hand. Joe signed with a flourish and slid both back to Farris.

"Now, Agent Farris, I am just dying to know why I am here."

"Let's cut the shit, Joe. You know goddamn well why I am here. 'Ol Jammer Franks got himself strangled across from a brownfield across town. You remember him don't 'cha? The only witness putting you in the strip mall in Kenosha where you bought the GPS that you used to stalk your wife before you strangled her, and the same make and model you used to track your former associate Jackie Dekker."

"Agent Farris, I believe Mr. Maxwell confessed to murdering my wife. He's not doing so well, from what I understand. Tick tock, tick tock. And if someone used a GPS to stalk Ms. Dekker, this is the first I am hearing of it. She is a bit of a floozy with some men and a you-know-what tease with others, if you catch my drift. Probably she picked up one too many frat boys, or dumped one too many Prince Charmings, and one of them couldn't handle that she is a love 'em and leave 'em type. She probably got the GPS herself just to accuse me. Ms. Dekker, while a lovely young woman, is far more interested in me than I am in her."

Farris snorted. "Oh really? The blonde athlete with the major league rack, looks like an underwear model, and has legs up to here, is obsessed with you? But you don't think she's attractive, is that it? She must have the hots for men over forty with thinning hair and a paunch."

Joe clenched his teeth. "I'll have you know I exercise regularly, Mitch. Maybe you should join me some time, look like you could use it."

Farris didn't take the bait. "You know how your wife Tina died? Strangulation. Same with this Franks kid. Oh, we also have an unsolved murder of a kid named Todd Perry. Went on a date with Dekker, who you probably jerk off to every night, and he was dead twenty-four hours later. Strangled, in case you haven't guessed. Hell of a coincidence, ain't it?"

Farris' accusation of three counts of murder did not sting Joe as much as the accusation—accurate as it was—that Joe self-abuses to the vision of Jackie Dekker. Joe hoped Farris didn't sense that it made Joe flinch.

"I am sure that I don't know what you are talking about, Agent Farris. But perhaps I can help you out. When was this Franks fellow killed?"

"You know goddamn well, Haise. Saturday night was the last time anyone heard from him, left his friend's apartment around nine o'clock to meet a Facebook friend. Oh, and the friend didn't exist. We checked the kid's message history; it was a fake account with pictures and everything. Someone lured him into a trap. Ring a bell?"

Joe rubbed his chin in a gesture implying deep thought. "Saturday night…Saturday night. Eureka! I attended some experimental theater at The Citadel. Bit of drivel, musical about siblings in a womb. I bought the ticket online; the receipt is at my house. The coat check girl was a shameless flirt, I am sure she'd remember me."

Farris responded instantly, almost as a reflex. "What was the opening number?"

"'The Fertilization Shuffle.' God awful."

Farris continued the rapid-fire. "What song ended the first act?"

"That was 'You Are So Lamaze-ing' performed by the chorus, the Trimester Troubadours. Would you like to know the closing number?"

"Unless you saw the entire play the week before and skipped out of Saturday night's performance, smartass. We're not that dumb."

"It was opening weekend, Agent Farris. Apparently, you *are* that dumb."

Farris slammed his folder shut and pounded his fist on the table. "Listen Haise, if you plead to the Jammer Franks murder, and I mean right fucking now, I'll forget about your wife. She was banging that guy, got what she deserved. *And* the Todd Perry murder will just go unsolved. *And* Franks was a Ritalin sniffer, no one will show up to court and demand you get life, you probably did society a favor with that one. Cop to it now, and you'll get fifteen to twenty years; I have the juice to make a deal, already cleared with Justice. You are getting fifteen to twenty for three murders; it's a fucking gift. But this offer expires in five minutes."

Joe shook his head and offered a *tsk-tsk*, as a parent might do with a wayward child that disappointed his father. "Mitch, Mitch, Mitch, whatever shall I do with you? I know what you think I did. But I have a solid alibi on the Franks matter. If you had any witnesses or prints, I'd be in handcuffs right now and you'd have an army of techs ripping my house apart. Maxwell pled guilty to my wife's murder, and I just can't help you with this Perry matter. Not one bit. Now, I am sorry that Jackie Dekker is upset that I wouldn't sleep with her and retaliated against me by making up an accusation that I stalked her. Just tell that filthy slut to close her knees and this kind of thing won't happen."

Farris' fist flew across the table and caught Joe across the chin. He crashed to the floor as his attacker upended the table. Farris sailed across the room and grabbed Joe's shirt collar, clenched his fist, and reared back. The door blew open, two agents burst in, and wrestled Farris out of the room before he could land a second punch. A third agent pulled Joe back to his chair and checked his face.

"You all right, sir?" The agent removed a penlight from his sport coat and flashed Joe's pupils.

Joe rubbed his chin and flexed his jaw muscles several times. "I'm fine, really. He isn't much of a brawler, I'm sorry to say."

After being tapped on the shoulder, the agent stepped aside. Joe was face-to-face with his boss, United States Attorney for the Northern District of Illinois, Dave Dunham.

"Ah, Dave. So good to see you. I trust you had nothing to do with this spectacle."

Dave, Joe's boss, was a flighty but brilliant man. The President appointed him as the US Attorney of the third largest city in the nation, a position one doesn't earn without a whole lot of brains. Dunham supported, and promoted, his loyal prosecutor as Joe struggled through his wife's murder, only to now suspect him of killing her and two others.

"Joe, you all right? Took a hell of a sucker punch there."

"Fine, Dave. Just fine. Now what about this charade? Accusing me of murder and whatnot."

Dave sat on the corner of the table. "You know how it is, Joe. An accusation was made; have to do our due diligence. But Joe, this looks awful. I am sure you can appreciate it."

"Dave, I can only appreciate that I've been off work for almost three weeks and I'd like to get back to the office. And not to put too fine a point on it, but I consulted with a labor attorney recommended by the National Association of Assistant United States Attorneys. He assured me that I can only be terminated for cause. Based on what has been going on with my suspension, unless I am going to be arrested and charged with some offense, I am entitled to have my job back. So, I am willing, because I have always been about the team, Dave, to overlook Agent Farris' felonious assault. I am true blue with our boys with the badges, though I'd check that man's mental stability. But I have hearings coming up in a few weeks on a number of my cases, so I really should get back to work."

Dunham leveled a hard look at Joe. As much as Joe knew he had control of Agent Farris, Dunham gave Joe a chill.

"I know all about that, Joe. The report will be complete in a few days, you'll hear from me the day after. But yes, you may ultimately be reinstated."

"Excellent! Now, when will Ms. Dekker be ready to go? I have a lot of work for her."

Dave's eyes opened wide. "What? 'When will Ms. Dekker be ready to go?' Joe, are you out of your mind? She's been permanently transferred to Springfield. C'mon Joe, are you that tone deaf to what's really going on here? You are never going to contact her again under any circumstances. And if you do, if she even sees you anywhere in Springfield, I'll fire you for cause."

For the first time, Joe inadvertently let his guard down. He visibly slumped in his chair and muttered "Springfield" under his breath. "Very well, Dave. Best to keep her away from me. She really ought to pursue men her own age, anyway." Joe stood up and scooped his coat off the floor.

"Alright, Joe. So long as you understand. CPD is going to take you home. I'll have the letter out to you in a week. If I order reinstatement, you can return a week from Monday."

Joe wiped a drop of blood from his lip as an officer escorted him out. A minute later, Farris walked into the interrogation and shut the door. Dave shook his head. "We're not going to find anything on him, are we?"

"Nope. Did you hear that alibi shit? I'll grab one of CPD's guys and we'll check it out, but guarantee he tried to bang the coat check girl just so she'd remember him. He either caught a rehearsal the week before or he paid cash for a ticket on Friday night just to make sure he saw it in case we asked. Then he slipped out Saturday right before it started, killed the kid, and slipped back before it was over."

"Think anyone will remember him Friday night? Or maybe someone saw him slip out Saturday?"

Farris shot Dunham a look that conveyed the point, *Did you really ask that stupid fucking question?*

Dunham nodded. "Yeah, I know. He isn't dumb. What about the coroner?"

Farris pulled out a cigarette, lit it and took a deep pull. Though strictly banned in all federal buildings nationwide, suspects loosened up when they smoke and the interrogation room was the one place that was unofficially exempted for high-value targets. Before he could put his pack away, Dave grabbed the pack from Farris' hand, withdrew a cigarette, and absent-mindedly tucked the pack in his own pocket. Farris lit Dave's cigarette but said nothing.

Farris exhaled a long pillar of smoke. "Coroner said Franks was strangled, but there were no definitive finger marks except bruising right at the hyoid. So Haise probably wore gloves, meaning we can't even gauge the size of the killer's hands. Evidence techs said no fibers, DNA, stray hairs, saliva, nada. Computer guys backtraced everything they can about the Facebook account. Know where Facebook's servers traced the IP address to?"

"Libertyville, Illinois? Please?"

"Sevastopol. It's in Russia. Or the Ukraine. I don't fucking know."

Dave blew smoke out of the corner of his mouth. "I have to hire him back, don't I?"

"I can't make a case by next week, Dave. I need at least a year. Not to mention, Chicago PD has jurisdiction over almost everything and isn't too interested in Haise unless we come up with something solid. So yeah, you have to hire him back."

Dunham shook his head in frustration. "I called the powers that be and convinced them that Joe may have committed some state and federal crimes that you stumbled into when investigating work-related offenses, you should be tasked to them to try to close out all three cases."

"What federal offenses are those, Dave?"

"I have no clue; I was improvising. But they bought it, so you have all the juice you need." Dave tossed his cigarette on the floor and crushed it out with his toe.

"At least you got to drill the little fucker."

Chapter 19

"Jackie? It's out. Check the web." Mavis popped her head in and out quickly, she was clearly excited. Jackie opened her browser and refreshed the website for the local paper.

In a case of truth being stranger than fiction, a Virgin Islands man was arrested when he was discovered carrying nearly two dozen endangered tree snakes at the local Greyhound bus station. Known alternately as "Horace" and "DJ Elrod St. Delacroix," he is charged with importing....

Jackie read the web article and wrung her hands. Most lawyers loved "profile," a nice little media ego-stroke, but Jackie had been there and she knew it simply meant everyone reading it had an opinion about her, which typically ranged from dismissive to downright vulgar. The worst online comments were from those who were obviously lawyers criticizing her legal tactics. Hopefully, no one would read this one.

The bail hearing the day before was uneventful, save for the menacing stare the defendant shot her way. Something about Mr. DJ Elrod whatever—*What the hell kind of name is that?*—made her uneasy. He was built like a linebacker and walked with the strut of a man who wasn't to be trifled with.

The defendant was released on a signature bond. The case is being prosecuted by Jacqueline Dekker of the Springfield US Attorney's office. When reached about the case, she declined to comment.

She closed the browser. *Yeesh, I hate that line.*

***

Across town, Horace made bail by listing a local address as his temporary lodging. No one cared too much about the name 'Louisa Breckenridge' in Springfield. Horace was in trouble, but not so much that the federal government was worried about him making his court dates. He first appeared in court seventy-two hours after being arrested; he was treated well and there was only a passing reference to his nickel-and-dime criminal history. The prosecutor, a delicious blonde with legs from here to there, caught Horace's eye. He hadn't seen a vision like that among the regulars back home. She was his executioner and muse all wrapped up in one tasty package. She seemed a little too eager to get him in trouble. With his history, his federal defender told Horace that he was looking at a few years in prison. That simply wouldn't do.

He caught a taxi and gave the driver Louisa's address. If she were really the sap he expected, she would love the surprise visit. And maybe he'd stay a few days, see what she had worth stealing. Mostly, he needed a base of operations to sort it all out. His lawyer mentioned that the prosecutor was new and from Chicago, had a tough rep, didn't like to plead out. "Still getting a read on her," he said.

Horace took the hint; she was a problem. He didn't like violence, but Horace couldn't do prison. Not at all.

The cab pulled up to Louisa's house in the late afternoon. Horace had barely slept, ate, or bathed since his flight. He struggled to put on his game face. He knocked gently and awaited an answer. An elderly woman in her housecoat peered anxiously from behind a curtain. Horace beamed and repeated his name several times until his hostess registered the name.

"Jamely? Dexter Jamely? Oh my! I thought I'd never see you. Come in dear! Please excuse my mess, I wasn't expecting guests."

Horace explained that he came from the Virgin Islands on business and was calling on local Christians. He could barely keep his story straight, but she was dim enough that it really didn't matter.

"Louisa, my child, may I freshen up? I just landed and haven't had a chance to rest up."

The old woman threw out a number of bible passages about offering shelter to those who need it.

Horace responded, "Ah, Psalms, of course. I know it well." She offered a brief look of confusion and led him to a small bathroom that needed work. He showered while she made sandwiches and by the end of the evening, he was settling in her guestroom. She had nothing worth stealing, but he would worry about that later. He was out as soon as his head hit the pillow.

Chapter 20

Jackie pulled into the hospital parking lot, climbed out of her car, and spent a minute stretching. She hadn't worked out as much as usual; the cold weather, the sparse fitness center at the hotel, and all the time she spent with Kevin eating his fabulous cooking didn't help. Maybe most women would've killed for her figure, but Jackie felt soft and it bothered her.

She crossed the lot to the main entrance and began checking to see if anyone followed her. It had been weeks since she'd felt Joe Haise' ominous presence, and she hated the sinking feeling she was getting. Detective Buddy Scott gave her a .38 snubnose pistol; she despised carrying it only slightly less than the thought of confronting Joe Haise without it. It sat at the bottom of a box in her hotel room, she considered dusting it off. *I hate this life.*

She made her way through the labyrinth of halls and color-coded elevators to a large wooden door at the end of the hallway. She tapped and entered.

"Mr. Maxwell?"

He looked at her with bright eyes. "Ms. Dekker! Come in, dear. My lawyer just left with my health care paperwork. Told them to pull the plug when the time comes. No sense having those damn shock paddles or some heavy orderly bust all my ribs with CPR, so he had me sign all the paperwork. Lawyers are the worst."

Jackie took off her coat and pulled up a chair. "Vampires, every last one of them."

They shared a laugh; Jackie opened her purse and pulled out a bag of green, seedless grapes. "Grabbed this from a store down the street, thought we'd have another impromptu picnic."

"Hooray! Let's eat, my dear. Time for another of our romantic dates. But you seem down in the dumps, tell me what happened."

Maxwell looked worse than before, but his spirits were high. Jackie spilled the beans about the murder and the likelihood that not only would Joe get away with murder, again, but he would actually get back to work.

"I am truly more offended that he is going to represent the United States government in a court of law than get away with murder."

Maxwell patted her hand. "I know. And I am more offended that his wife is lost in all of this, that he won't ever face true justice for that. I don't have much time left, Ms. Dekker. But I wanted to see him account for what he did."

"It would be nice if you could be publicly cleared, Mr. Maxwell."

"Not for me, dear. I don't care about my legacy. For Tina. She deserves justice."

They ate in silence and Jackie had taken to holding his hand. He squeezed back but, keeping with the sense of respect, neither commented on it. Maxwell possessed and conveyed dignity and reverence to her; he never made an inappropriate comment, sexual innuendo, or dirty joke. They were somewhere between a father and daughter and a mentor and protégée. Though they both knew that Maxwell spent time with Tina Haise because she was a hooker and he liked paying for sex with a young pretty woman; discussing it in such crass terms was a line neither would cross.

"Mr. Maxwell, what did you enjoy most about Tina?"

He gobbled a grape and thought about the question. "She was unbelievably silly. Not just funny, but *silly*. She could imitate a Donald Duck voice like nobody's business. You've seen her picture, girl-next-door face, honey blonde hair, and the cutest dimples I've ever seen on a petite ballerina's frame. Imagine such a girl talking like a cartoon character. She made a comment once, we were lying in front of a fire, sipping wine, and she said she never got to do goofy things like that at home. I think she regretted saying it the moment it left her mouth. I just hugged her close and said, 'Shhh. Be vewy vewy quiet,' in my best Elmer Fudd voice. We both laughed ourselves silly. God, she was so beautiful. And I was so young and strong. I aged ten years in the last five. It may sound crazy, but if she were here, I'd be healthy. I think cancer is my punishment for letting her go. If I had any courage, I would have whisked her away from her bastard husband and helped her start fresh someplace. Maybe I would have divorced Veronica and married Tina. Or maybe introduce Tina to some of my young single brokers. She sure deserved some happiness."

Jackie nodded her agreement. "I read a file about her when I was researching the case. She was misunderstood, I think. She was an introvert, came from a broken home, no father and her mother was a little nuts. She had no close friends, no pictures of her at a big birthday party or anything. Joe mistook her solitude for subservience, but I think she was just thoughtful. I don't envy her that she felt being an escort was her only escape, and I am sure it took all she had to put herself out there."

Maxwell agreed. "She and I never went out; I assumed she didn't want to be noticed. Though maybe she hated crowds but tolerated them only when she had to, like when she was fundraising. But in an intimate setting, she was a totally different person, she was free. We danced together in my house, I told her I could waltz but she didn't believe me. I told her I would teach her, and every time we met, we'd cook dinner, dance the Waltz, then make love. She trained as a ballerina when she was younger but never did the waltz. She told me one time that she practiced at home alone because she loved it so much. I just hope that she felt something for me, that it wasn't just a business transaction."

"Mr. Maxwell, I never met Tina but I am certain I know her better than her own husband. I'm convinced of that. But I didn't know she could do a Donald Duck impression or that she yearned to learn to dance the waltz. I think she felt for you too, and I wish she could have escaped *him*."

They sat in silence and took turns wiping away tears. After the last of the grapes disappeared, Jackie tucked the bag in her purse and stood to leave.

"I'll be back next week, you take care of yourself."

"I will, Ms. Dekker. And don't let that bastard get the best of you."

Jackie leaned in and kissed his forehead. "I won't Mr. Maxwell. Promise."

Jackie walked out and closed the door behind her. She made her way back to the car, checking all around her to make sure she was safe. *Even a paranoid person can have real enemies*, she thought.

Gary Maxwell could still smell Jackie's perfume in the air; even though his twin daughters were the light of his life, his ex-wife squirreled them away in Europe and it became increasingly evident he'd never see them again. But Jackie's very presence made him feel that one person on the planet loved him. He was exhausted; the meeting with his lawyer and Jackie took everything out of him. He smiled as he settled in for a nap, but he felt something was off. He opened his eyes and looked into the face of evil.

"Hello Gary."

Chapter 21

Joe could tell that Gary Maxwell's blood ran cold. Joe sat next to him for a full thirty seconds before he opened his eyes.

"Wakey wakey, eggs and bakey."

Maxwell hissed. "You bastard. What do you want?"

"Gary—can I call you Gary?—It's been so long since we spoke the day you were sentenced for killing my beloved whore. Wife. Whatever."

Maxwell narrowed his eyes and his demeanor soured. "You are a two-bit hustler with a law degree, Haise. If you came to me looking for a job, I wouldn't bother to use your resume to wipe my ass. You aren't good enough for a woman like Tina, you never were."

Joe removed a syringe from his pocket. "Now Gary, do you really want to start there? We are getting off on the wrong foot." He waved it about and placed it back in his pocket.

Maxwell noticed for the first time that Joe was wearing a white doctor's coat. He'd clearly bypassed the visitor desk for this visit. His body slackened. "Fine, we can shitcan the petty insults. Let's assume we're both past that now."

"Good. Now Gary, I don't relish being the harbinger of death. I view it as an occupation. There are simply people on this planet who really shouldn't be. They consume oxygen that the rest of us could put to much better use. And the ironic thing is, five years ago, you would have agreed with me. Admit that much to yourself." Joe stood and began to circle the bed. He studied the monitors and IV bags as he pontificated. "Take you, for instance. I prosecute slick money-changers like you every day."

Maxwell sat up and barked, "I never broke the law, Haise. And you goddamn well know it."

"Oh, maybe not the federal law. But you broke the natural law. You, my dear Gary, plowed your seed into my crop. You should know you don't plant your rhubarb in another man's garden without consequence. And I'd like to think your little sideshow here"—Joe gestured toward at the array of medical equipment and drugs—"could be the universe rendering judgment on you for violating that law."

"You know, Haise, whether you do me now or the doctors do me in a week, none of it matters. You know why?"

"Oh, do tell."

Maxwell displayed a peaceful smile. "Because your wife loved me and I loved her. And the last night of her life was spent in my arms, not yours."

"Ha! That's because the check cleared, Maxwell. She was a hooker. You don't think she loved you, do you? You are a sap."

Now it was Gary's turn to laugh. "You are the sap, Haise. Yes, she was a pro, but you know full well she enjoyed every minute with me. She would have done it for free. And it burns you."

Joe withdrew the syringe, held the tip up to the light, and squeezed until a single drop of viscous liquid oozed out. Maxwell knew he could do nothing to stop him. He was too weak and Haise wasn't someone to feel pity.

"I am here, Gary, because I am working my way out of that little mess you created with your courtroom antics. It has not been easy, even for someone like me. It takes cunning and patience, but I need to make sure I have covered every angle. And that's where you come in."

"Are you saying you need my help? Fuck you. There's your help."

"*Tsk tsk*. Language. I am here to make sure that, one way or another, you don't do anything else to screw this up worse than you already have. See, Gary, you gave a statement and now you are going to be interviewed under oath on video. They are probably working to convene a grand jury right now. That's what I would do. And you will be asked over and over about our little unspoken arrangement. And I know you managed a way to spirit your trophy wife out of the country someplace. So, I don't have leverage there, we can both admit that."

"You'll never find her. And if anything happens to me, I've made arrangements to make sure she knows that it was you that attacked her that morning on her jog. She would spend every last penny she has to bury you. I may be sick, but she has more balls than both of us and she could go the distance with you. She'll finger you in a heartbeat, swear she got a good look at your face. Don't even think about it."

Joe cocked his head in disappointment. "Now Gary, you did no such thing. 'Oh, I made arrangements that information will be disseminated if anything happens to me, blah, blah, blah.' You've seen too many mob movies. So, save the hollow threats, she holds no interest for me anyway."

"So what, then? I keep my mouth shut or you kill me? Looks like that is on the menu, anyway."

Joe inserted the tip of the needle into the IV port and placed his thumb on the plunger. "You know, Gary, I have been waiting for this moment for so long. I wanted to hurt you, punish you for what you did. Every night after I discovered Tina's little secret, I would lie in bed next to her and imagine her wearing some ridiculous outfit, standing in front of someone like you, doing every vile thing you asked, and I fantasized about all the ways I could castrate you. Watching you go to court, go to prison, taking your money, it just wasn't enough."

Joe stood over Gary, holding the power of life and death in his hands, letting the moment linger. He let a small, evil laugh escape his lips. He looked into Maxwell's eyes and winked. He withdrew the plunger and secreted it back into his pocket. Maxwell donned a puzzled expression at his tormentor.

"Do it! What are you waiting for?"

Joe cracked his knuckles and stepped away from the bed. "I suppose there *could* be an autopsy and this little gem *could* be detected in your bloodstream, though it is unlikely. But I really should hedge my bets and let Mother Nature finish the job. So here is what we are going to do. I'm not done with you yet, but I need to ensure your silence for the rest of your miserable days, or else I will make sure you to suffer more pain than you could ever imagine one man can endure."

Maxwell was defiant in his tone. "I don't care what you do to me, Haise. Everyone sees through you now. You're all done."

Joe crossed the room and paused as he turned the doorknob. "Gary,

I know you care for our little blonde harlot. And if you get amnesia and let nature take its course, then you and I are quits. But if you even think about talking to the cops or that pudgy little shit from the Inspector General's office one more time, then I want you to know that, in your waning days on this planet, I am going after your little protégé. What we will do together, Gary, it will be Biblical. And when I am through with her and my hands are wrapped around that delicate neck of hers, listening to her moan her last breath in my face as she begs me to finish her off, I am going to whisper to her that it was all your fault for not playing ball. I promise she is going to curse you with her very last agonizing breath. I want you to know that."

With that, Joe slipped out. Mustering the little energy that Gary could muster, he screamed as loud as a dying scarecrow could.

"Haise! Haise! Get back here! You bastard!"

Chapter 22

"Ms. Dekker. Can I call you Jackie? You can call me Hector."

Sigh, I hate the false congeniality that comes with this job. "Of course, Hector. If we're going to take your client to trial, we might as well get comfortable here." *Cue the plastic smile.*

"Now, Jackie, we both know that you have all kinds of proof problems. And what I like about these conferences is the chance to show our cards."

Why, when he says my name, does it sound like he's scolding a truant child? "I'd like that, Hector. Let's get it all out and see where we stand."

"Great. Because my client has a loving husband and family and she wants to put this matter behind her. My sole focus here is ensuring that we can reach a plea agreement."

If that is your sole focus, then stop staring at my tits. "Well, let's review what got us here in the first place."

Proffer sessions are often used by federal prosecutors and defendants to talk about what help a defendant could offer the prosecution that would result in a reduced or dismissed charge. These conferences are preceded by the parties signing a proffer agreement, also called a "Queen for a Day" letter, because all parties promise that anything said will not be used in the prosecution. The target can admit to criminal activity and it cannot be used against them at trial. However, nothing prevents the prosecution from using information gleaned at a proffer session to pursue a derivative case against the target. *Oh, you said you conspired with Lee Harvey Oswald? We didn't have that. Now we do. Thanks, asshole.*

But if a defendant is pretty well screwed, the proffer session can be a way to convince the federal prosecutor that there is a bigger fish in the pond and only they can help catch him. And naturally, every defense attorney is trying to hustle as well. *I'm telling ya, you thought Enron was bad? These guys are worse! And my client has all the cards. This is gonna make your career, buddy. I smell a judgeship in your future.*

Consequently, the cubic feet of bullshit spewed in a proffer session can get pretty deep, pretty fast. But considering that federal bullshit is usually measured in metric tons, it wasn't so bad.

Maisie Mae Anspaugh was born and raised around Peoria. She was a hundred and ten pounds of dynamite with a personality bigger than her pocketbook. She was nicknamed MMA, after the mixed martial arts professional fighting organization. She was petite—a whisker over five feet tall with short fire engine red hair in a bob—and a ball of energy. She knew everyone worth knowing and everyone adored her. She would show up to a cocktail party and work the room, shaking hands, sharing inside jokes, and dropping bits of gossip about the Springfield social scene, to the extent there was one. She was a lioness at the Capitol, making sure the right people met the right politicians.

No one was actually sure what Maisie did for a living. She was a registered lobbyist, but she boasted only a few clients, including the Central State Sugar Beet Growers Collective and something called the International Fraternal New Order of Cartographers, which advertised itself as "The premier organization dedicated to exposing the inherent racism and classism in maps produced by the traditional map cartels." No one bothered to ask how Maisie made money, she just did.

One night last summer, a female intern for the Governor was asked to deliver some documents to the home of the Illinois Speaker of the House. She knocked on the door and a voice yelled out, "Come on in! We're ready!"

The intern, a junior Poly Sci major at the University of Illinois, walked in to see Maisie in the living room on all fours, with the Speaker on his knees mounted behind her while his leggy blonde wife lounged naked in a nearby chair. Apparently, they'd been expecting the House Minority Leader and his wife to round out the evening, in an unprecedented display of bipartisanship.

It was a glorious scandal. The minority leader, who campaigned on a family values platform, claimed he had no idea that his presence was expected at an orgy on the evening in question and he was offended by the implication. He added that his wife would be spending the remainder of the season at their summer home in Ypsilanti, Michigan.

The Speaker of the Illinois House of Representatives suffered a vastly different fate when the news splashed all over the Chicago Tribune. When pictures of his wife, a former Weather Bunny for Chicago's Action 8 News Team, was juxtaposed with a picture of Maisie in her college dance team uniform, his favorability rating jumped six points.

The affair would have ended there if not for the efforts of a gossip blogger site who dug around Springfield, pulling expense reports and calendars for state officials acquired under Illinois' Sunshine Law. The reports showed a lot of legislators and aides spent a lot of time meeting with Maisie, both in their offices and at some of the finer gin mills in Springfield, Chicago, and even twice in Washington, DC. A number of unnamed sources claimed Maisie used her God-given assets to gain access to people in power, then used her God-given talents to gain influence. Or as one source put it, "Her figure got her the meetings and her knees got her the legislation." A few organizations were rumored to have paid substantial consulting fees to Maisie, indecipherable groups with names like, "Freedom For Illinois," "Freedom From Illinois," and "Illinoisans For Freedom."

One of the groups that retained Maisie's services was called, "Rural Voter Rally," a 501(c)(3) non-profit—and tax exempt—organization whose sole stated purpose was to increase voter registration and participation in rural America. Because rural America voted for Republican presidential candidates nearly 70% of the time, it was no shock that the group was funded by a billionaire owner of an Evangelical Christian media empire. When Illinois passed bills to fund mobile voter registration vans to travel to rural counties two years earlier, Democrats were mildly irritated that the Republicans stole a page from their playbook. When Maisie's antics hit the front page, Democrats were outraged that her fingerprints were all over that piece of legislation. An investigation turned up evidence that Maisie was skimming from the group by invoicing them for equipment she never purchased and rental space for offices she never leased. The tawdry sex and undue influence in the Springfield Statehouse gobbled up newspaper ink, but all Maisie did, as far as the feds were concerned, was not declare some income on her annual tax returns. To the press and the public, the tax evasion charge was lame, but to Jackie and her colleagues, it was good enough for Al Capone.

Her attorney was Hector Mayhew, a middle aged and somewhat respected solo practitioner with a home office in Decatur. Maisie couldn't spring for anyone better; her bank accounts were all tainted with the odor of illegality so she wisely hired the best—and cheapest—lawyer she could reasonably claim she could afford.

The purpose of the proffer session was Hector's attempt to convince Jackie that Maisie could bring down the Illinois legislature. Surely, an offer to repay all back taxes, plus penalties and interest, would warrant dismissal of the evasion charge, in exchange for such valuable assistance. However, the defendant didn't just have to provide assistance to the feds to receive such consideration, they had to provide *substantial* assistance to get the deal. And Jackie was skeptical Maisie had anything that juicy to offer.

Also in the meeting was an accountant from the FBI named Louise Barker, a rather frumpy woman that never smiled and always wore stockings and black Crocs, a fashion offense greater than any crime she was investigating.

"I think I'll ask Special Agent Barker to direct the interview, Hector. It will be more methodical than if you or I manage it."

Hector nodded enthusiastically. "Exactly! That's exactly what I was thinking. We should have Louise conduct the interview."

Hector was acting a little goofy, which was not that unusual from what Pops Logan told her before the meeting. Jackie started to suspect Hector had a little whisky bracer before the get-together. But boredom was already creeping in, so she ignored her suspicions in the interest of getting the hell out of there as fast as humanly possible. She and Hector both fired up their laptops. Jackie could take notes and, if something Maisie said didn't add up, she could quickly reference the FBI FD302 field reports and witness statements.

"Ms. Anspaugh, as Ms. Dekker indicated, I am Special Agent Barker, and I'd like to go over some of the things that you have to offer. Let's start with how you became involved with Rural Voter Rally and began an attempt to influence legislation for your client. On the evening of...."

Snore. This is so goddamn boring. Jackie noticed Hector had checked out and was looking at his computer while his eyes drooped. Jackie received a popup, indicating an instant message from Kevin, with a personalized tag.

Boyfriend!: Hey! It's me. I'm bored. Have to design a skateboard park. I hate skateboards. Talk to me.

She looked around; Maisie was still recounting her lobbyist filings and client meetings. She subtly typed a response.

You: In a meeting. Bored too. When do you get back from Chicago?
Boyfriend!: Got extended a day. Be back this weekend. I'm horny.
Jackie blushed. *Stop it, I have to concentrate. :)*

Kevin could IM faster than Jackie, especially when he was feeling frisky. *Boyfriend!: What are you wearing? ;)*

She shifted in her seat and made brief eye contact with everyone before returning to her keyboard.

You: Black stockings, heels, skirt, and a blazer. Now leave me be!
She knew she was only encouraging him.
Boyfriend!: What are you wearing underneath all that fabric?

Jackie began to perspire, brushed her hair behind one ear, casually studied the people in the room, and typed a response.

You: Black bra, black boyshort panties. Why are you asking, you naughty boy?
Kevin's responses were coming faster. *Boyfriend!: Oh gawd, that is hot. I am having some difficulty here.*

Jackie stifled a giggle. Something Maisie said brought her attention back to the meeting.

"I can tell you, Agent Barker, the first time I slept with a legislator, was with Senator Jack Mayhew. It was just after I was hired by Rural Voter Rally, we call it RVR. I met Jack at a cocktail hour sponsored by the NRA. We talked about voter outreach."

Barker interrupted. "Did you pay for Senator Mayhew's drinks that night? Or maybe the NRA gave him something of value? Steak dinner? Maybe a door prize?"

Maisie laughed. "God, no. He insisted on paying for everything. He is a straight as they come. Well, about most things, anyway."

Damn, Jackie thought. *Almost had something there. Need a good crime or this is a waste of time.*

"What happened next, Ms. Anspaugh?"

She paused and took a sip of water before answering. "It was the night of that big storm we had two years ago. Jack told me he really appreciated my work for the party, then he complimented me on my eyes. I told him I remembered his wife was really sweet when I met her; she died in a car wreck the year prior. He was struggling to raise his daughter alone. We talked about baseball, he played for the White Sox for two years and I said that he looked like he was still in playing shape. Then he smiled, which was kinda sweet."

Maisie was right. Jack Mayhew was an Adonis: Six-foot two with thick, wavy blonde hair and blue eyes that sparkled even in a dark room. Women around town would joke that if he pierced you with those eyes, you'd melt. On top of that, he was Norman Rockwell sweet: a doting single dad, a tolerable moderate Republican, and a restaurant-quality chef in the kitchen. Every woman in Springfield wanted Jack Mayhew. Jackie promised herself that if he would ever switch political parties, Kevin would have to wait in the on-deck circle while Jack Mayhew took a turn at bat. She drifted off into space and created the mental picture of Maisie and Jack in an upscale Springfield bar. *A few drinks after a late night, a lingering look, she rests her arm on his... Is it getting warm in here?*

Another IM popped up. *Boyfriend!: Hon, I want to nibble your neck. Can I get you out of those stifling clothes this weekend?*

Jackie began to glow; she hoped it wasn't obvious. She crossed her legs and squirmed uncomfortably in her chair.

You: Stop it! I can't concentrate. You are going to get me in trouble.

Agent Barker broke Jackie's concentration. "What happened next, Ms. Anspaugh?"

"Jack knew the NRA wanted to do a lit drop and their lobbyist asked me to take a look at the brochures. As we were talking, lightning struck and we lost power in the club. Everyone started to cheer, waitresses brought out extra candles, it was fun. Anyway, he grabbed a candle and guided me into a back room to get the materials. He fumbled for the door and we stepped inside the office. Then he set the candle on a desk and looked into my eyes. He touched my cheek and—"

"Ms. Anspaugh, did any of the materials from the NRA mention the RVR? Or did the NRA pay for the RVR's promotional literature?"

Shut the hell up, Louise, this is getting good.

"No, the NRA is even more anal about compliance than Mayhew."

Barker furrowed her brow. "Very well. Continue."

"He pulled me close. We began to take off each other's clothes and were kissing like crazy. He ripped a button off my blouse when he tore it open. We couldn't wait, and he cleared off the desk. Then he pulled me...."

Boyfriend!: I want to pin you to the wall and peel off your panties.

Jackie swallowed hard. She noticed for the first time her breathing was shallow. She felt her mouth go dry as she messaged back.

You: I want you inside me, Kevin.

"We started to make love on the desk, but people were starting to drift to the back of the bar so we stopped and got dressed. He invited me to go someplace more intimate and I said yes, we were like two teenagers. So, we ran out of there and flew down the highway to the Hilton and got a room. We started peeling our clothes off in the hallway and barely made it in the door when we started up again."

Jackie got goosebumps and caught herself staring at Maise's petite hands. She imagined those fingers running through Jack Mayhew's hair, grasping a fistful and pulling his head into hers for an intense, red-hot kiss. Those very hands, not five feet away, held Jack Mayhew's perfect face. *So not fair.*

Louise broke her train of thought. "And who paid for the room, Ms. Anspaugh? Did you pay for it? Or maybe he used his State-issued credit card?"

Lady, you are really killing the vibe here.

"He put it on his personal credit card."

Between Maisie and Kevin, Jackie moved from perspiring to sweating and was not-so-subtly writhing in her seat. *Are we almost done here? Is the heat in this room broken?* Jackie began to unconsciously fan herself with a folder. She pushed her chair back from the table. "I just have to make a call in the hallway. Please keep going, it should only take a minute."

Jackie slipped into the ladies' room and splashed cold water on her face. She quickly messaged Kevin, *You: You are in trouble, young man. Report to my bedroom this weekend for a spanking!* She fixed her hair and straightened her skirt before heading back into the conference room.

Fortunately, they were back to the mundane subjects of the day. Maisie managed to keep it PG while she discussed finances and political organizing. Louise was oblivious to the gold mine laid before them and continued to fish for information. By the time Maisie was ready to explain how she ended up naked on all fours about have sex with a number of like-minded individuals, Jackie had cooled off.

The meeting wrapped and Jackie promised Hector she would call. Jackie escorted them both out, shut the door, and flopped in her seat.

"Well, Agent Barker, that was a total waste."

Louise flipped through pages of notes. "Agreed. Maybe a few meals or drinks were paid for that shouldn't have been, but that's it."

"Keep in mind, Louise, that we are being asked to help nail some of the most powerful people in the state, if not the country, for doing things that may be completely legal. I am not sure RVR did anything wrong, or that any money went where it wasn't supposed to go. I'm sorry, but I am not sticking my neck out for this baloney."

Louise nodded. "You and me both, sister."

Jackie packed up her things and stood to leave. Agent Barker thanked her and stood as well.

"Say, Jackie, can you believe all that tawdry dime-store romance novel stuff she copped to? I mean really, fooling around with Senator Mayhew on a desk in the back of a pitch-black bar? Then tumbling into a hotel room half naked? Group sex on a living room floor? Who could imagine doing such things?"

Jackie furrowed her brow as she stared off into space for several moments. "Hmm? Oh, I'm sorry, what was the question?"

Chapter 23

Lake Forest is a wealthy suburb north of Chicago. It is slightly more affordable than Winnetka, but if one has to ask how much more affordable, look someplace else. Joe did his homework when he selected the tavern that would serve as his hunting grounds a month prior. When he was conducting online research and stumbled across The Snare, he laughed, chalked it up to serendipity, and hopped in his car. It was a short fifteen-minute drive from Libertyville, but he utilized his counter surveillance measures and it took nearly an hour. Deerpath Road runs East-West and ends a few hundred feet from Lake Michigan. Naturally, every shop along the boulevard looks like something out of a movie set, almost too good to be true. Sharp red brick façades, perfectly manicured flower boxes, bright green awnings, and nary a Taco Bell drive-thru in sight. The Snare's website indicated they had an immediate opening for waitstaff and bartenders. *Perfect*, Joe thought. *Whether they hire someone in the meantime or not, spending a busy Saturday night at a bar that is either understaffed or has brand new servers is great way to blend in to the background.*

    Although Joe managed to settle out of court with Gary Maxwell for Tina's death—Joe always smiled when he imagined Gary Maxwell signing the check, with all those zeros and commas, Pay To The Order Of The Man That Murdered My Mistress And Hung Me In A Frame—he was careful to stash the proceeds into several conservative investment vehicles, with a monthly check for the dividends as his play money. But that evening, he would allow himself to spend freely at an upscale restaurant, with a menu of ridiculously expensive cocktails, in the company of an even more expensive lady of the evening.

    He spent the afternoon surveilling the area, memorizing the route, and imagining every scenario from the need to make a quick getaway to where he could imperceptibly dispose of something if—or when—the need arose. He located the street and slowed his pace to a crawl; it was full of Mercedes and Audis, but Teslas were becoming the new plaything for the rich and powerful and even Joe had to marvel. Though he could afford one, he would not allow himself to surrender to such impulses. Joe was playing the long game with his money. Though he permitted himself one extravagance tonight. He spied The Snare just ahead on his left, made a mental note of the parking availability, and drove on.

He proceeded to drive several blocks east until Deerpath ended at Lake Road, with the shores of Lake Michigan no more than fifty yards beyond. He turned left and drove north for a quarter mile until he spied a turn-of-the-century farmhouse facing the Lake. It sat on five acres of some of the best real estate in the Midwest. Joe pulled in to the circular driveway, past a short white picket fence surrounding the property. In the summertime, this would certainly be an expensive night indeed, though the rate for a single Saturday night in winter was only slightly less obscene. Joe stopped in front of a flight of white wooden steps leading to a wraparound porch. He spotted ceiling hooks that would support a porch swing that was obviously in winter storage. A large barn sat in back of the house, the website advertised horseback rides along the lake for their guests. Though a casual observer might balk at paying $750 for a single's night stay in a farmhouse, this was the going rate for rustic-chic in Chicago. The B&B featured a James Beard winning chef and was touting its recent inclusion in the Michelin Guide.

Joe marched up the stairs, through the etched glass wooden doors, and into the lobby; he was greeted by the aroma of chocolate chip cookies mixed with a roaring fire in the fireplace. The receiving room looked every bit the one-hundred-fifty-year-old working farmhouse as advertised, though the decorator admirably added every modern luxury convenience without ruining the rural aesthetic. A voice called out to his left.

"Welcome to The Harbor Home. How may I help you?" A middle-aged woman greeted him from behind a sprawling cherry wood antique desk. Made without much of a thought a hundred years ago, it was worth thousands today. She was not attractive in the traditional sense, but she exuded professionalism. A crisp navy blouse, short black hair, and a pair of glasses resting on a sharp Roman nose. She appeared as one would expect of the proprietrix of one of the most expensive B&Bs this side of the Mississippi.

"Yes, good afternoon. I have a reservation for the evening. I'd like to check in now so I don't need to bother with it later tonight."

"I can certainly understand that. The name of the reservation?"

"Jim. Jim…Maxwell."

Joe suppressed a smile as she scanned a monitor. "I have it right here, Mr. Maxwell. I see you prepaid the reservation." Joe nodded, The Harbor Home's website allowed him to secure the reservation online with a $5,000 prepaid Visa gift card, though it bore no name.

"I will need to see a credit card for incidentals, though."

Joe anticipated this. He pulled out his wallet. "Miss… I'm sorry, I didn't catch your name."

"It's Marie."

"Marie, so glad to meet you. Now, I would rather just pay cash. Perhaps I could put something on retainer for incidentals." Joe peeled of five crisp Benjamins. "See, Marie, I don't really need the guys at the Exchange knowing where I brought my girlfriend. And can I have a room in the back? I don't want to disturb the other guests when I head out early tomorrow. I will just do the auto checkout and you can simply donate whatever is left on my account to the Illinois Equine Rescue Association. Can we do that?"

Marie's very professional and reserved front cracked ever-so-slightly. "Oh my, I think we can make that accommodation, Mr. Maxwell. Our horses here are so well treated, but others aren't so kind."

Joe slid the bills across the table. "I know that, Marie. In fact, the Harbor Home's reputation in the animal welfare community is why I chose to stay here."

Marie was beaming as she handed over the room card, map of the grounds, and a brochure. Joe smiled, bid her adieu, and headed back home. He pulled into his driveway in the late afternoon, warmed up a mug of tea and fired up his computer, careful to cover his cyber tracks when he was doing something he knew he shouldn't. Well, *society* says he shouldn't send the email he was about to send. But who the fuck gave society the right to judge someone of such professional and personal accomplishments as Joe Haise? No one, that who.

He opened his dummy email account and began to type.

Hi Victoria! It's Jim and Tisa! Can't wait to see you tonight. Tisa will be a bit late, her closing is coming down to the wire. But I'll be there. We'll be meeting at 7:00pm at The Snare on Deerpath Road in Lake Forest, I'll attach a map to this email. Looking forward to meeting you at last! We'll have some drinks and a bite to eat, then back to the B&B for a romantic evening. Remember, Moet & Chandon always tastes better naked. ;)

Joe stripped and jumped in the shower, repeating his body shave ritual. Yes, he was going to enjoy this evening. He picked out a Navy blue Brooks Brothers blazer and yellow paisley silk tie, gray slacks and Italian black leather shoes. Joe laid out his wardrobe on the dining room table yet again, using packing tape to remove any stay hair or fibers. Satisfied, he completed his evening beautification routine, dressed, and gave himself one final look in the mirror. He smiled, winked at himself, and headed out, stashing the packing tape in his pocket. *May need this later*, he thought to himself and chuckled.

***

"I'll have the Cobb salad with vinaigrette on the side."

"Very good, miss. That comes with a side of our seasoned home fries, garlic mashed potatoes, fruit salad…."

Jackie didn't hesitate. "Fruit salad." The waiter laughed, he was her age and cute. She could detect when someone flirted with her, laughing too hard at her jokes was a dead giveaway.

Kevin smiled and shook his head. "Always on the health kick with you. I'll take the cedar plank salmon and roasted red potatoes. And we'll take another splash of wine."

The waiter smiled at Jackie and stepped away. "Kevin, I am getting soft, the gym at the Residence Inn is not the greatest and my friends at work keep taking me out for lunch. The gang is complicit in my laziness."

"Hmm, your 'friends at work'? The 'gang'? You never said things like this about your colleagues in Chicago."

"Wow, you're right. I hadn't realized that." Jackie had to ponder that one.

"Except for your homicidal pervert of a boss."

"Except for my homicidal pervert of a boss, correct dear. You are right again."

"Don't sound so shocked, I can be right once in a while."

Jackie laughed, "Kevin dear, if this relationship is going to work, you have to realize you are never right."

He raised his glass, Jackie took hers, and they clinked. "I stand corrected, dear."

Jackie took a healthy swallow, her second glass of wine was causing her to feel flush. They sat in the back of a rustic Italian joint; most of her neighbors preferred Outback or Appleby's, any kind of chain restaurant in a strip mall. But a small authentic stand-alone place like this was popular with Chicago refugees like her. The tables were miniscule and their knees practically touched under the table, but on this night, it was the most romantic place in the world.

"And another thing, stop sending me naughty messages at work. I can't concentrate in a meeting if I am turning beet red because you made me horny. And you haven't rocked my world in almost two weeks, I was in a vulnerable state. So knock it off."

"Oh Jackie, we both know that's not going to happen. So you should probably just get used to it."

Jackie didn't normally say things like "horny" and "rock my world" in a crowded mid-price Italian restaurant in the heart of Springfield, but the combination of the wine, Kevin's flirtatious emails from the day before, and her inability to stop picturing Jack Mayhew making love to Maisie Anspaugh eroded her filter. She was also doing her level best not to imagine what Maisie felt like when Jack grabbed her, ripped open her blouse, cleared the desk in a fit of passion, and mounted her as she grasped fistfuls of that perfect blonde hair. No ma'am, she wasn't going to think about that scenario at all.

Dinner arrived and Jackie devoured her salad. They giggled throughout the meal and made more than a few double entendres. Clearly, Kevin had been feeling their sexual drought as much as Jackie was. By the time their plates were cleared, the alcohol sufficiently wore down Jackie's resolve to the point that she agreed to share a sorbet dessert with Kevin. The waiter reassured her, "Miss, it is really low fat, cross my heart."

He left and Kevin held out his hand, Jackie took it. They smiled at each other; Kevin could always crush Jackie when he stared into her eyes. She slipped off one heel and extended her leg under the table. Kevin's expression of shock let her know that she found pay dirt when her toe slid under his khakis and reached his bare calf.

"Hon?"

"Shh." She began moving her toe farther up her leg. Her eyes were half closed and she displayed a Cheshire Cat grin, the byproduct of a full, satiated appetite. She removed her foot from his pant leg, he briefly donned an expression of relief. It was short-lived, as Jackie pressed her stocking-clad foot into his crotch.

"Whoa!" Kevin, coughed and tried to speak. Jackie uttered another, "Shh" and began flexing her toes. Now they were both sweating.

***

"*Victoria?*" Joe waved across the room, mouthing the name of the woman he was expecting. Well, the name the woman gave him, he would best every last penny of Gary Maxwell's money that it was fake.

She pointed toward the bar and thanked the hostess as she walked toward Joe. She was tall, nearly six feet in heels. Her raven hair fell to her shoulders, which were bare and toned. She wore a backless black dress with, as advertised, a deadly slit up the thigh. Her breasts were nearly perfect, and she made sure her cleavage caught the attention of whomever she passed. Her chestnut-brown eyes shone from across the room and more than a few husbands tried to surreptitiously catch a glimpse as she sauntered by, careful not get busted eye-fucking the woman Joe Haise would have on his arm. He loved every bit of it.

"Jim, so glad to meet you at last. Victoria Chase." Joe stood as she stepped into him, gave him a kiss on the cheek, and a lingering hug.

"Victoria, the pleasure is all mine." Joe spent hours trying to find just the right girl. There was no shortage of websites offering company for the evening. Joe despised most of them. The women offered their disgusting bodies for fifty dollars an hour at a hotel room near the airport, and they had names like Cinnamon and Alexxxis, no class whatsoever. But Victoria was different. She charged three thousand for a full evening, twice that if she spent the night. She spoke French, painted watercolors, and her favorite opera was *La Traviata*. She enjoyed sports. She was perfect. She was Jackie Dekker.

"Victoria, Tisa called and she can't make it. She may join us later, but her deal is falling through and she needs to spend the night settling the clients down. But please, let's have a cocktail and talk."

She placed her clutch on the bar and sat next to Joe. She promptly crossed one toned leg over the other, revealing the edge of the seam of her stocking. Joe swallowed hard.

"Victoria, I do recall that you noted that you always appreciate a gift, and I've never met a woman that didn't love this brand." Joe handed over a small, elegant gift bag with the tell-tale tartan pattern across the front.

"Aw, Jim, you shouldn't have." She placed her hands on the gift bag, Joe could make out a faint indentation in the skin of her left ring finger. She carefully opened the bag and removed a slender women's wallet. It was tan with black and white vertical stripes at either end with red intersecting lines across the front. Classic Burberry. She unzipped the pouch, opened the flap, and maintained an even expression as she spied a bundle of one hundred dollar bills tucked inside. She expertly ran a thumb over the bills and fanned them for a quick inspection. She muttered under her breath, "*l'appel du vide.*" She closed the flap, zipped it shut and replaced in the gift bag.

Joe smiled, *a professional, indeed.*

"Merci, Jim, it is just perfect. You are such a charming man. I only wish Tisa was here. I hope we can meet her later, I am sure she is as beautiful as you are handsome."

Joe beamed. *This beautiful woman that turned every guy's head in the room told me I am charming. And handsome. And did you all get a look at her gams? Thigh-highs, gentlemen. Take note: they will be on my bedroom floor later.*

They ordered cocktails and Joe requested the chef's sampler. The bartender brought a cutting board containing a variety of fruits, nuts, and exquisite cheeses. Joe could not stop staring at this stunning creature, but he reminded himself this was a transaction and required a measure of detachment for everything to go as planned. Still, he couldn't help gazing at the top of her stocking peeking out at him. After she brought her arm to rest on his, she leaned in and whispered, "Jim, please. You know you want to. Don't be so bashful." She took his hand off the bar and placed it carefully on her knee. He slowly moved his thumb back and forth, caressing her leg. His lips trembled ever so slightly. They talked for half an hour; Joe could barely remember anything she said.

"Victoria, you are absolutely lovely. And cultured, but I must ask about your background in athletics. That fascinates me. What sports do you play?"

"Well, I like to do yoga and Pilates. I also tried my hand at cheerleading in high school, but the tumbling wasn't something I was born for. Otherwise, I just played volleyball."

Joe's jaw fell open. He could hardly breathe. "Volleyball? Did you say you played volleyball?"

"Oh, yes. I played in college down south at an SEC school."

Joe nodded to the bartender. "Check, please."

***

"Jackie, the dessert is on its way, we can't do this here."

"I feel naughty. And no one can see anything." She could tell her foot was having an effect, Kevin was getting aroused. The waiter chose that very moment to arrive with their sorbet.

"Three flavors of sorbet, raspberry, peach, and lemon. Enjoy."

Kevin was nodding intently to the waiter while Jackie's foot was dangerously close to causing an all-out crisis in Kevin's slacks. The waiter thankfully departed.

Jackie took a spoon and casually took a bite; her foot never stopped moving. Kevin ate twice as fast, struggling to avoid both a brain freeze and an orgasm. He finally had enough and called for the check. As the waiter approached and handed the folder, Kevin was already shoving bills at him and telling him no change was necessary. He spent a few moments adjusting his pants and stood, hoping the other patrons weren't paying too close attention. Jackie found her shoe, slipped it on, and joined Kevin in a near-sprint to the car. He peeled out of the parking lot and sped toward the apartment while Jackie unbuckled his seatbelt, unzipped his fly, and began playing with his stick shift while he was trying to avoid an accident, both on the road and in the car.

They arrived at his apartment, nearly broke down the door, and began leaving a trail of clothes to the bedroom. He was on top of her within minutes.

***

Joe pulled into the Harbor Home and drove to the back of the main house. Victoria followed him in her car, Joe insisted they take separate vehicles to make sure she felt comfortable. She cooed over his concern for her feelings, then quickly accepted his offer.

He walked to her car and opened her door as she shut the engine off. She drove a late model Infinity, black with all leather interior. *She must be doing well on her back*, he thought. He casually observed a sticker in a corner of the windshield that read "Park High School Faculty Parking." Joe held the door as she stretched her leg stretched out and she stood. He was aroused and couldn't wait to show her what he had in store. As he closed her door, he spied an empty juicebox on the floor in the backseat.

He led her to the back door; they quietly entered and walked down the hall. Her heels on the hardwood echoed off the walls, the loud clacking noise made him cringe. He needed stealth, not a parade. They arrived at the door to their room; he swiped the card and entered. He found the light and shut the door behind Victoria as their eyes adjusted to the light. The room was striking. Though it had the bones of an old farmhouse bedroom, it exuded five-star lodging. Fresh cut flowers, plush towels, robes and slippers, and a large four-poster bed with a billowy white goose-down comforter. There was no mistaking this for anything less than the best North Chicago had to offer. Victoria let her coat drop to the floor, threw her arms around Joe's neck and kissed him. He was stunned; he did not expect her to take the initiative. *Perhaps I don't know my own magnetism*, he thought.

"Victoria, take your clothes off. I want to make love now." She offered an expression between confusion and amusement, surprising a woman in this line of work was pretty damn hard.

"I have to freshen up first, honey." She grabbed a lipstick case from her clutch and excused herself. Joe fumbled with his clothes, furiously stripped to his birthday suit, and turned down the sheets. He noticed her clutch lying unattended. He bent an ear toward the bathroom; she was still running the faucet. He scooped it up and unsnapped the case. Sitting majestically on top was a white gold wedding ring and a packet of three condoms. *Naturally*, Joe thought. He flipped through bits of random makeup, a cellphone, and a small red leather ID case. He checked for movement again, the faucet was still running. He opened the small folder. *Pictures...two kids, whatever. Husband, meh. Probably a sap in bed. Costoco membership. Illinois driver's license...name...name...Amy Druckleford, age 29*. He paused, arched his eyebrows, and looked toward the bathroom door, whispering, "Well hello, Amy. Cute last name, who's your daddy now, Amy?" He offered a brief *tsk, tsk*, replaced her clutch, and climbed into bed.

She emerged from the bathroom wearing a black lace bra, garters, stockings and matching panties. She tossed her hair and looked seductively at Joe. "Ready for me, tiger?"

Her beauty stunned him, he could only mutter an, "Uh huh." She crossed the room and slid in bed beside him. Within minutes, Joe was on top of her.

Victoria clearly knew her job, she was calling "Jim" and moaning at all the appropriate times, but Joe knew she was putting on an act. But there, in the middle of nowhere, where no one even knows who he is, who she is, he was free to do anything.

Joe offered a thrust. "Do you like this, Jackie?"

"Oh yes, Jim. I do."

Another thrust. "Yes, Jackie. Tell me you want me. Tell me you are a whore."

"Yes, Jim. Your Jackie is a whore, a dirty whore. I want you so bad."

Joe's hands slid up her body, across her firms breasts, to her delicate throat. He placed both hands around her neck. Another thrust.

"You want this, don't you? You want me to do it, don't you, Jackie?"

"Oh yes, Jim. I want this. Do me, I am your dirty girl, Jim."

Joe began to squeeze her throat. She began to choke. Joe thrust faster. Victoria began to thrash, Joe squeezed harder and moved faster. Her face contorted. He screamed, "Oh God, oh yes! Oh God!" Victoria's eyes began to bulge, her face began to turn blue as he squeezed harder. Her expression turned to pure terror as her eyes rolled back in her head.

"Oh God, Jackie!"

***

"Kevin, do me. I want you."

Kevin needed no instruction; he was into Jackie as much as she was into him. They were moving as one; the wine, the sexual drought, they could barely contain their lust.

"Oh God, Jackie. You are so hot right now."

She moved her hips with him and began moaning. "Oh God, yes. You like this, baby? You want me?"

"I want you Jackie, you are my sexy girl."

Jackie held his head tight against her neck, her legs were wrapped tightly around his hips. She was on the verge.

"Mm, I'm your naughty girl. Our waiter tonight was cute, he was flirting with me. I bet we could have so much fun together. You both could ravage me. Would you like that, baby?"

Kevin continued to thrust but could barely respond coherently. "Yes, yes baby. Whatever."

"Yes, so hot. Both of you kissing me, tearing my clothes off. Yes, honey, I'm your naughty little girl. Fuck me, Kevin. Oh God, Kevin. Don't stop!"

They climaxed together, screaming in unison as they released the pent-up frustrations of weeks spent apart, days spent flirting with each other, and the days Jackie spent wallowing in the tawdry details of Maisie's sex life. For a full two minutes, they rocked their bodies in unison as they expended every bit of energy they had, finally collapsing in a sweaty heap. After five minutes of panting, Kevin spoke first.

"Wow. That was…unbelievable. So, is this one of those times we won't talk ever again about the, um, dirty talk at the end?"

Jackie was too mortified to open her eyes. "I don't know what you're talking about. Now shut up."

***

Joe relaxed in bed, peaceful in the moment. He couldn't recall the last time he was this content. A prone, motionless figure lay next to him as he casually thumbed through her clutch one final time, considering his next move as he learned about his latest conquest. *Amy Druckleford…Amy Druckleford… married mother of two, school teacher, unusual last name…whatever will I do about you, Amy?* Once in a great while, the planets align, the river card makes the flush, and the sun shines on those who truly deserve it. Lying in a five-star B&B, at last scratching the itch that plagued him for far too long, basking in the afterglow of wanton lust, Joe was truly blissful. Knowing Miss Victoria Chase was really Missus Amy Druckleford was a bonus, discovering something that was not supposed to be known thrilled and empowered him. Particularly someone with such a unique name. He replaced her things and settled back in bed, shutting his eyes.

The figure next to him, minutes after hovering near death, finally stirred. A wavering voice broke the silence, "I don't think I want to work with you again. Please don't contact me."

Joe didn't move, or even open his eyes, as she eased out of bed and scrambled for her clothes. He casually murmured, "Leave the stockings on the floor."

"Victoria" scooped her shoes and coat and slipped out of the room in a half-zipped dress. Once on the other side of the door, Joe could hear her struggle to get her heels on in the hallway as she quietly sobbed. Minutes later, Joe heard her car start and squeal out of the parking lot.

What's her problem? Could have been worse for her, you know. She is quite lucky I found her so pleasing. And $3,500 for a cocktail and an hour of her time, including the tip? That's more than any school teacher makes, that's for sure. Hell, that's more than any lawyer makes. And the wallet was another five hundred, so I really don't see the problem. Women…can't live with 'em, can't live without 'em.

Chapter 24

The call was brief. Dave Dunham made minimal small talk before telling Jackie the news wasn't good. He was forwarding her more detail, though it was "....against his better judgment." It would explain everything, he said. He sounded defeated, but reassured her that Joe would still be prohibited from contacting her or travelling to Springfield. They hung up and she waited for the alert from her computer. After what felt like an eternity, a ding from her office desktop broke the silence.

    Forwarded from David Dunham, US Attorney, Northern Dist. of Illinois, Eastern Div.
    Orig. email below:
    To: David Dunham, US Attorney, Northern Dist. of Illinois, Eastern Div.
    From: Baruch Goodman, DOJ Office of the Inspector General
    Re: Joe Haise matter
    Dave –
    My full report will follow tomorrow. After an exhaustive investigation by Agent Farris, I can report at this time that I cannot advise that you empanel a grand jury to investigate Assistant US Attorney Joseph Haise. There is little to implicate him in any traditionally federal offenses. Staff has worked extensively with Detective Buddy Scott and the Cook County District Attorney. There is a disagreement with local au-

thorities over whether Joe Haise actually murdered his wife Tina, the witness Jammer Franks, or Ms. Dekker's acquaintance Todd Perry. Though we all agree there is insufficient evidence to charge him with those offenses. Frankly, with the untimely demise of Mr. Franks, any semblance of at least a stalking case against Ms. Dekker evaporated. Agent Farris spoke with Mr. Maxwell, he was evasive and, honestly, he is terminal at this point and won't survive much longer. I am no labor-law attorney, but I can certainly understand why Mr. Haise feels he is entitled to his job back. At this time, I cannot offer any evidence, even under a reduced civil-service burden of proof, that would give cause to terminate his employment. I will continue to monitor the situation and I am sorry I could not offer any more definitive conclusion to this saga. I hope an alternate solution will present itself.
Bingo

Jackie slumped in her chair. No matter how well she prepared herself mentally for it, the ending was still a gut-punch. *So that's it. He's coming back. Sonofabitch beat 'em all.* She closed her computer, shut down, and headed out for the night. She stopped by the desk and told Mavis she wasn't feeling well. Before long, she was on the road home. She made a few stops for gas and some groceries—including a bottle of wine that, if there was a God in heaven, would render her totally inebriated in short order. Her feet ached and she couldn't think of a good reason she was still in this line of work. Something else nagged at her—she felt as if she were being followed.

After the Joe Haise debacle, she confronted her paranoia and learned to control it. But she couldn't shake it this time. An old beater car seemed to appear and disappear, but it didn't *feel* like Joe Haise. Didn't seem to be his style, too passive. And now that he was about to be reinstated, he wasn't going to shoot himself in the grapes by doing something so brazen and stupid.

She arrived at the hotel and hauled her grocery bags to the room. She kicked off her shoes and stretched out on the bed. She sent a text to Kevin telling him about Joe and that she needed some space tonight. He was empathetic and understanding, he told her he loved her.

She took a hot shower, polished off a tray of sushi and the better part of the bottle of wine. She was asleep in minutes. Later in the night, could've been a minute after she closed her eyes or maybe an hour, she woke hearing a creak in the floorboards. Jackie could have sworn she saw a shadow under the door emanating from the hotel hallway, but the wine was hard to shake off and the specter was gone a moment later. She fell back into a fitful asleep.

The next day was not much better, though burying herself in work served as a fine coping mechanism. Kevin vowed to make her a romantic dinner, rosemary crockpot chicken with steamed carrots and potatoes. She drove home from work but felt the same sense of dread. She changed and showered before meeting Kevin for dinner. As she walked around the room grabbing clothes, she could swear someone was outside the door of her hotel room. The light behind the peephole darkened momentarily—was she seeing things? She quickly finished dressing, grabbed her purse, and stepped carefully into the hallway, but saw no one.

Paranoia was becoming her new normal and she struggled to ignore her instincts as she drove to Kevin's. An hour later, she forgot all about the creaks and shadows and settled in for a casual evening. Weekdays she went back to her hotel, it was too hard to make do in the morning with Kevin; they had different body-clocks and morning routines. She made it back home and crawled into bed just before midnight. But the sense of impending doom intensified, this time she could swear the door handle to her room jiggled. It wasn't subtle.

Someone was watching her. He was there. Or they, could it be a 'they'? Joe Haise was not this indiscreet. Kevin was too sweet. If he had a dark side, she would have picked up on a vibe by now. This is something else entirely.

The creaking floorboard and the metallic rattle of her door was enough to rouse her from her fog. Jackie eased her arm from under the blanket and stretched across her body to the nightstand, until her fingers found purchase with the crosshatched handle of the .38. The looming presence paused momentarily and stepped away from the door. Jackie's heart beat rapidly as she paused with her hand on the butt of the gun.

What if it was a guest who simply got the wrong room? What if I shoot some poor husband who got off on the wrong floor?

She withdrew her arm, but left the drawer open. Once again, she would get no sleep. It wasn't until she arrived back at the hotel lobby after work the following evening that it all began to spin out of control.

"He said he thought he clipped you in the parking lot yesterday when he backed out. Asked for your room number so he could deliver his insurance information, I didn't give it though." The hotel clerk was sweet and adored Jackie. He was no more than nineteen and thought he had a shot with her, so he was always on the lookout. She was registered under the name of Janet Ross for security reasons; consequently she had to remember to respond to 'Janet' when he flirted with her, which was nightly. He said the man occupied the room down the hall from hers, checked in a few nights prior and checked out an hour ago. He said her visitor was a black guy and spoke "kinda funny." She got the chills and considered the only funny-speaking black man she knows: St Delacroix.

She still had the number of the US Marshal back in Chicago that checked her in the very first night she was spirited away from her evil boss. Everyone called him "Hoss" and he was the kind of law enforcement that was bored to death and prayed every day for a reason to pummel someone. She dialed him right away and parroted the account from the clerk.

"I don't think this has to do with Joe Haise," she added.

Hoss assured her it was fine, he and a partner would check on Haise to verify he was in Chicago, he would then call the Springfield office and have a team roust St. Delacroix and see what the story was. They would head to the address he listed on his bail forms and would have an update within the hour. The call came sooner than that.

Chapter 25

The team of US Marshals rolled up to Louisa Breckenridge's modest home about a half hour later. Had they arrived an hour earlier, they would have been there in time to prevent Joe Haise's latest masterpiece.

Joe was monitoring his favorite subject, Assistant US Attorney Jacqueline Dekker's spectacular body. A day earlier she wore a black skirt that rode up her leg as she climbed out of her car; she then dropped her keys on the pavement and bent over to scoop them up. Joe saw the waistband of her panties peeking out from the small of her back. G-string. He needed a full five minutes to recover from the vision. He considered briefly what a municipal charge of public masturbation would mean for his return to duty status, but decided he could wait to take care of personal matters until later. Although he was banned from entering the Springfield City limits, he decided in that moment that geography was a bullshit artificial construct and that he would weigh the consequences of violating his hundred-mile radius at a later date. Besides, he was on paid leave, who the hell was Dave Dunham to order him to stay away from the State of Illinois' capital? Joe might have pressing business with the Governor about another pending indictment—Illinois Governors seemed to get a lot of those. He managed to tail Jackie to a Residence Inn downtown. It was there, late one night, he spied Horace.

Horace was skulking around Jackie's car, lurking around the hotel, and basically acting like an annoying little shit. Joe followed Horace as Horace followed Jackie. Once Jackie arrived at work, Joe trailed Horace to Louisa's house. Horace was dumb enough to keep his legal papers on the front seat of his piece of shit car and, fortunately for Joe, Horace didn't lock his car door. The vehicle registration was in the name of an old woman, but this Horace fellow seemed to be monitoring all of Jackie's movements for the last few days. He spied a note at the bottom of a page of chicken-scratch that read, "need shovle and lime."

Lime? It's lye, you dumbass. You dissolve a body in lye heated to three hundred degrees. Jesus. No, this certainly won't do. Not…at…all.

Joe knocked on the front door and introduced himself to Horace as someone from the US Attorney's Relocation Amnesty Partnership Exchange. He presented his credentials and, stifling a laugh, explained the RAPE program was designed to help select defendants obtain new identities in a location of their choosing at the conclusion of the case. Horace, too happy to bother with the absurdity of the story, invited Joe inside, turned his back on his guest, and walked to the living room. He took a blow to the back of the head with a tire iron and collapsed to the floor in a heap. Joe's belt was off and around Horace's neck in moments. Five minutes after knocking on the door, Joe was in his car on the way back to Chicago.

***

The Marshal called his supervisor in a panic; the supervisor called local PD and Roz Jeffries. Roz called Jackie.

"Wait, Horace is dead? How?" Jackie was in shock.

"Blow to the noodle and strangled. Now I know what you are thinking, but this is not *him*. For one, Horace had a laundry list of bastards that wanted him dead. Second, it wasn't the only murder. The home belonged to Louisa Breckenridge, she was the dead guy's local contact. We are still looking into how they met, but it is probably a Good Samaritan thing. She was found dead as well, suffocated with a pillow. Horace had her car keys in his pocket and her dresser drawers were rifled. Looks like she's been dead for days, Horace was using her place as a base of his smuggling operation, we think."

"So, was it him at the hotel?"

"It was Horace, all right. Hoss found a bunch of things in the vehicle with your name on them. Routines, parking spot, etc. Sorry to say, but it comes with the territory, Jackie. I am ordering twenty-four-hour protection for you for a week. But Horace has no other local known associates and we think his smuggling connection killed him to keep him quiet. Believe me, you are the last person his friends want to see. They are in the wind."

Jackie thought Roz was doing an admirable job of selling her bullshit theory. "Roz, I can't do this. I mean, really? What the hell kind of life am I living? Do all federal prosecutors go through this?"

"I hate to say it, but yep. Talk to my old underling who nailed those biker gang one-percenters a few years back. He still rides his bicycle every day because he fears a car bomb. So, Mr. DJ Horace Elrod St. Delacroix is room temperature, no crying over spilt milk."

She shook her head and began to laugh. "I forgot about the DJ Elrod part." She laughed harder. Then Roz joined in. Soon they were both in tears. Jackie sighed, "Roz, I am all out of tears. Laughter is all I have left."

"I get it, I really do. I will have the guys follow you for a while until we are back into the routine."

Jackie thanked her and said goodbye. She could hear Roz mutter, "DJ Elrod" and begin chuckling again as she hung up.

Chapter 26

He whistled into the receiver. "Jesus, Jackie. What the hell have you gotten yourself into?"

"I dunno, Nate. Sorry, Your Honor. Or is it My Lord Sir Knight of Judicial Realm?"

"A pox on your house! I will close you in my fist and smite you down, strumpet!" In their days working together in Chicago, Jackie would offer Nate a friendly ear; she was the only one could talk to about his relationships, hiding his sexuality from his grandmother, and the shame of it all. He was elevated to the federal bench shortly before Jackie's world fell apart and, proving fate wasn't all bad, they wound up in the same place anyway.

"You are mixing your genres again, Nate. Shakespeare wasn't quoted in the Bible."

"That's because the God took a 2,200-year break in between inspiring Samuel and Billy Shakes."

"Listen, dinner tonight, my place. Ernest is dying to meet Mr. Bikepath. Eight o'clock, sound good? I'll text you the address."

"Love to, see you then."

Jackie texted Kevin, who was thrilled to receive the invite. Time out with Jackie was in short supply as of late, but this was his first time meeting someone in her orbit. He offered to pick her up outside the hotel at a quarter to.

Kevin arrived in the hotel lobby; the young, cute, and obviously in love hotel clerk eyed him with suspicion. Kevin knew enough to nod the Marshal staked out in the lobby and ask for "Ms. Janet Ross."

Jackie stepped off the elevator. Even when she dressed casual, she caused Kevin to lose the gift of speech. She wore skinny jeans and red sneakers, a white oxford shirt underneath a red cardigan sweater with the sleeves partially rolled up, and a thin, silver necklace—a gift from Kevin after the first time they had sex. They laughed about it then and now, he fumbled through an explanation the night he presented it, "I don't know what the hell I was thinking, okay? You gave me the best sex of my life and I thought I supposed reward you somehow. I'm a guy, we're not that bright." She wore her hair in a ponytail, a touch of soft red lipstick, and her tortoise-shell glasses. Her glasses always made Kevin melt, the whole "I've got the body of an underwear model but I'm also smarter than you" look killed him—and she knew it.

"Wow, you take my breath away every time I see you."

"Thanks!" She smiled, gave him a hug, and stepped back to survey her man. "Let's look at you. What, no cargo shorts tonight?"

"No, smartass. You threw my last pair in the garbage." Kevin wore khakis, tan suede shoes, and a blue V-neck sweater. She looked him over, pronounced him "adorable" and they left arm-in-arm. They managed to make it to the car before she attacked him. After five minutes of kissing and thirty seconds of exploring what lurked behind Kevin's zipper, they decided they needed to get moving before things got out of hand. Jackie spent the drive reapplying her lipstick and fixing her hair.

They pulled up and Kevin reached into the back seat and withdrew a covered dish and a bottle. "Chardonnay and a dish of baked brie. I think they pair well together."

"Interesting. I usually pair my Chardonnay with a pint of Haagen-Dazs and regret, but this works too." They walked up to the door of a wonderfully landscaped Lannon-stone home in one of the nicer areas outside Springfield. She wrapped her arm around Kevin's waist, her grip intensified as she rang the doorbell. Nate answered with a huge grin.

"There is my fair maiden!" He scooped her in his arms, Jackie released her grip on Kevin and melted into Nate. They were both at home in each other's arms. "This must be Kevin, come on in. I can't have Jackie's noble squire freezing out there."

They stepped inside, the entryway was large and inviting; Ernest stood behind Nate like a meerkat, bobbing up and down, waiting for Jackie to make the introductions. Jackie met Ernest several times, enough to share a few giggles about Nate. He was an interior decorator, and quite a successful one at that. Despite having to move his business from Chicago to Central Illinois when Nate received his judicial appointment, Ernest adapted immediately. Gone were offerings of imported Italian marble and neoclassical finishings that were more at home on Lake Shore Drive, replaced with Amish handmade furniture and natural hardwood flooring more suitable for the tastes of the rural rich. In just about one year, he had more business than he could handle and had recently expanded his consulting business, taking on an assistant and advertising on local radio.

They sat in the living room, enjoying Kevin's brie and wine, making small talk and catching up. Kevin fit with the group like a glove, he and Nate talked college football while Ernest showed Jackie around the house. They made their way to the dinner table where Ernest dazzled with Asian pork loin roast and sautéed vegetables, roasted red potatoes and a strawberry vinaigrette and blue cheese green salad. Nate served a bottle of exquisite pinot noir and the laughs became louder and the pleasant conversation turned a bit blue. By the time they dove into a baked apple-raisin torte, their merry little band was in full swing.

They laughed about the culture shock of Central Illinois and the looks that Nate gets when he and Ernest hold hands. Jackie told stories of her first weeks on the job, Pops Logan, and the untimely end of DJ Elrod St. Delacroix. The name alone had everyone gasping for breath. Finally, Kevin accepted Ernest's invitation to retire to the kitchen and do the dishes, where he was promptly subject to a whispered volley of, "So when the hell are you gonna propose to that girl?"

Jackie and Nate finished the rest of the third bottle of wine and talked quietly.

"Nate, this was wonderful. I forgot how sweet Ernest is, you are so lucky."

"Thanks, and Kevin is perfect for you. Sweet, handsome, and he dotes on you. Ohmygod."

"You think?"

"Jackie, he wouldn't stop holding your hand, touching your shoulder, filling your glass. That boy is in love."

She smiled, "Yeah, I guess he is pretty sweet."

"You gonna marry him, or what?"

"He has to ask me first, Nate. And maybe. I think I'll let him twist for a while…before I say 'yes.'" He let out a squeal, she shushed him and they laughed themselves silly.

The darkness that hung over them all evening was still there, Nate was the one who broke the seal.

"What about Joe Haise? I hear he's going back to work."

Jackie took a healthy slug. "Yep, that's what Dave told me. He still has a work-issued restraining order keeping him away from me. If I see him here, he's done. But—"

"But he isn't that dumb, he isn't coming here. Which I suppose is good."

"Right. Nate, he murdered his wife Tina. And Todd Perry, that guy I had the horrible date with. And then they investigate him and I find that damn GPS on my car. And the only witness putting him at the spy store turns up dead? No freaking way, Nate. And I bet my student loans he had something to do with Delacroix, I can just feel it. Who knows how many people he's killed? He's a sick twist."

"That's not all. What do you think he's willing to do to get ahead at work?"

She furrowed her brow. "What do you mean?"

"Well, come on. He's ambitious; he has no conscience. What would he be willing to do? Destroy evidence? Manufacture a case? Blackmail? What's that to him when he already committed a whole shitload of murders?"

"You think he fixed cases?"

Nate drained the last of his glass. "Remember the Pep McDowell case?"

"Sure, politician took bribes to help fix a highway contract. That's the case that made you famous back in our office. Wait, you saying Joe had something to do with that?"

Nate's mood turned dark. He paused for what seemed like an eternity before he shook his head and cleared his throat.

"Jackie, Joe helped me on that case. Well, he more than helped. See,

Joe Haise—"

"Hello kids! Anyone want a dessert cocktail?" Ernest burst in with Kevin in tow; they were laughing and casting sideways glances as if they shared a wonderful inside joke. Oblivious to the mood in the dining room, they waited for an answer. Nate spoke first.

"Hell yes! We were both saying we needed one. Now let's have a final nightcap before these two have to go."

Nate stood and followed them to the kitchen, Jackie sat bewildered at the table. *I'm too drunk, what the hell was that about? I have to go home and sleep, I'll talk to Nate later about this.*

Kevin opted for a mug of chamomile tea to sober up for the drive; the others imbibed a Bailey's Irish Cream. After two healthy sips, Jackie forgot about Nate's comment and they all laughed until they could hardly breathe. Kevin and Jackie made it to the door and shared a round of hugs and promises to do this again. Jackie could have sworn Nate looked as if he was about to cry as she walked down the cobblestone path.

Jackie was playful on the way back to her hotel. They snuck in a back entrance in order to avoid the smitten desk clerk. They giggled as they tumbled into her room and enjoyed an hour of drunk, caution-to-the-wind sex. It wasn't until the next morning they realized they managed to gouge out a piece of plaster from the constant, furious banging of the headboard into the wall. The neighbors, if there were any, must have thought the Bears were holding a scrimmage in the next room. Kevin sported a perfect bloody bite mark on his shoulder and Jackie had nuclear-grade rug burns on her knees. They dialed up room service, Jackie fished some aspirin from her purse, and they spent the morning in bed recovering.

"Kevin, let's never do that again."

"Mmph. Wait, the drinking or the circus sex?"

"The drinking, dummy. We are doing the circus sex again tonight, so rest up."

Chapter 27

Gary nodded to the night nurse, "Alright, on your way then. Just needed you to dial, not listen to my life's story."

The nurse whom Gary secretly called "ignorant trash" behind her back muttered an "Mm hmm," and stormed out. He held the receiver to his ear, and it took all the strength he had.

"So it's all set then. Signed, sealed, delivered, so to speak…Yes…Yes…that is exactly how I want it. Did you send the email? Yes, and all the cc's as well. Don't you worry about why, that is my business. Good day, Counselor."

Gary dropped the phone on the bed, muttered, "Rat bastards, every last one of them," before passing out cold.

***

Jackie was reviewing Horace's file and preparing a motion to dismiss the charges. He was deader than a doornail and although the judge could read a newspaper as well as anyone, the federal courts ran things by the book. The case had to be formally dismissed due to the untimely, but societally beneficial, death of the defendant. That was when she noticed the email and cocked her head in confusion.

```
    To: David Dunham, US Attorney, Northern Dist.
of Illinois, Eastern Div.
    From: Louis Xander Dalrymple, Dalrymple &
Streicher
    Cc:  Joseph Haise, Asst. US Attorney
```

Jacqueline Dekker, Asst. US Attorney
Mick Halloran, Chicago Tribune
Stacey Delaney, CNN Host of "Keepin' It Real"
John Roberts, Chief Justice of the United States
Octavio De la Guardia, UN Commission on Human Rights
Re: Criminal Abuse of Prisoner
Mr. Dunham—

I am writing to inform you I represent Gary Maxwell in a civil capacity. My client tells me he is sick with terminal cancer and is treated poorly by the Bureau of Prisons. He is a patient at a hospital but cannot even receive something as basic as extra ice cream. Is this how you treat your inmates? He was also a witness in a recent case and may have even more information to share. But why should he do so when his nurses constantly call him a "douchebag?" Is that how we treat inmates in this country? I ask you, sir, who is the real "douchebag" here?

Please conduct yourself accordingly,
Louis X. Dalrymple
Dalrymple & Streicher
We'll Fight the Man & Keep You Out The Can!

Jackie stared at the monitor. *Okay, what in the ever-loving Christ is that about? Gary could care less about his conditions, he is terminal for Christ sake. And what is that offer to be a witness about? And why is he being represented by some ambulance-chaser? Has he lost his mind?*

A few emails between Jackie and Dave, accompanied by WTFs and question marks, indicated he was as confused as she was. Dave advised he called Dalrymple, who said that the email contained all he needed to know and that he would dismiss all potential civil claims in exchange for one hundred thousand dollars and at least once dish of ice cream a day.

Dalrymple then hung up.

Jackie tried to shake off her confusion and focus on work. It nagged at her the entire way home and as she lay in her hotel room trying to sleep. *What the hell is he doing?*

***

Nearing midnight, Gary Maxwell drifted between sleep and pain; the attending upgraded the morphine pump to Dilaudid, but he could barely withstand the agony. Cancer sucks, no two ways about it. He clutched the blankets and winced with each new jolt of pain, the bouts seemed to last longer each time. He finally felt some ease as the machine beeped and euphoria briefly filled his head. He heard the door creak, but kept his eyes shut as he spoke.

"Took you long enough, Haise. Where the hell have you been?"

"Hello, Gary. I must say, you look like hammered dog shit."

Gary briefly opened his eyes and glanced at his guest. "How did you like my invitation?"

***

Jackie tossed and turned, it was all so random. *And why did he cc: Joe Haise? Does he have a death wish or something?* She paused and held her breath, sat bolt upright, and scrambled for her phone.

***

Haise pulled up a chair and sat. "I thought the ice cream was a nice touch. Who the fuck is Louis Dalrymple?"

"Argo Nunya."

"Come again?"

"Argo fuck yourself, Nunya fucking business."

Joe shook his head. "Gary, we really can't keep meeting like this. In fact, I'm positive we won't."

Gary smiled through his pain. "I am gonna nail your ass to the wall,

Haise. Just wanted to tell you that. I am going to testify, video before the grand jury as soon as they get one empaneled. And I'm calling your bluff, you won't touch a hair on Dekker's head, she's too much woman for you. Sayonara, jerkoff."

Joe's gloved hand reached into his pocket, withdrew a syringe and placed it into Gary's IV port. "No, I think it is sayonara for you, Gary. Sweet dreams. Hope Tina was worth it."

Joe quickly pushed the substance through the port, withdrew the empty syringe, and stood. He shook his head with a twisted smile, replaced the chair, and walked to the door. He could swear he heard his victim mutter, "She was," as he left.

***

Jackie screamed into the receiver, the duty nurse at the ICU had to repeatedly ask her to calm down.

"Miss? I'm sorry, you are calling about who?"

"Maxwell, goddamnit! Gary Maxwell! I'm from the US Attorney's office. Is he under guard? What's his condition?"

"Ma'am, he is not under guard, he can barely move. And we checked him just a little while ago, but I can check again if that would make you feel better."

Her condescending tone infuriated Jackie. "Yes, please! Do it now!"

The wait was interminable, one minute turned to five. Then she heard a commotion on the other end of the line. Jackie was too late.

"Miss, I am terribly sorry, but it appears he passed away in his sleep. Do you want to—"

Jackie hung up and cried.

***

Roz and Jackie sat in Roz' office, Jackie's eyes were bloodshot and the entire office was abuzz with Maxwell's death.

"I talked to the Chief Medical Examiner in Cook County, Jackie. He said tox would take a few weeks but considering how bad off Maxwell was, a hard sneeze could've killed him."

"Roz, it was too perfect. Jesus, I'm telling you, he did it."

"Well, his ex-wife ordered him cremated, no memorial service. So that's that. And the ME said if he used potassium chloride or succinylcholine, it would be masked by everything else he was on. Gary had so damn many chemicals pumping through his system that the panel won't be able to tell the difference between what's supposed to be there from what was introduced."

"I know, Roz. Joe would have thought this out well in advance. You know what the worst part is?"

"What's that?"

"Seeing that email yesterday, it makes so much sense now. It was a red cape to a bull. Gary was tired of living and needed Joe's help to die. He was in so much pain, but he still had his wits. Sonofabitch actually managed to commit suicide."

Chapter 28

Joe's phone rang, he picked up after the fourth ring.

"Hello?"

"Joe, it's Dave Dunham. Just calling for two reasons."

"So glad to hear from you, Dave. What can I do for you?"

"One, I am calling to tell you that you are to be reinstated. Be here bright and early Monday to assume your caseload. However, the no-contact order with Jackie Dekker still applies. That is my rule, and I have the Attorney General's personal okay that you are to stay the hell out of Springfield."

"Well, Dave, I suppose that is acceptable. Though I hope she has a good mentor, she needs guidance during this difficult transition. I've been thinking about it, and I will need two good interns and at least another one and a half full-time positions. I want to ramp up prosecutions of some of these internet financial scams. I think there is some real profile in this for us, Dave. No one has gone after these guys in a concerted way and I think the press would really benefit the office."

Dave extended a raised middle finger to the receiver and muttered a non-committal, "Mm hmm."

"Great, I think it's a real win-win, Dave. Now, anything else can I do for you?"

Dave paused, as if to gather his courage. "Gary Maxwell passed away in his sleep twelve hours ago; you are on the victim notification list, obviously."

"Maxwell was an adulterous bastard, he can rot in hell," he hissed. Appearing to catching his mistake, he paused and added, "Oh, and also a murderer."

Dunham rolled his eyes so hard it was practically audible. "Yes, Joe, a murderer too. Now I have one final question for you."

"Shoot."

Dave Dunham heaved a sigh into the line. "I can't believe I have to ask this, but can you account for your whereabouts last night?"

***

Jackie gave Kevin the wave-off after Gary's death. She told him she needed time to figure it out. He'd learned long ago that Jackie, growing up poor and mostly alone, internalized her grief and processed it all on her own schedule. He loved her enough to give her all the time she needed. Days turned to weeks before she decided to allow herself to feel vulnerable again. After a brutal week at the office, and occasional bouts of crying quietly in the bathroom stalls at work, she reached out to him, asking if he could come by the hotel for dinner.

Jackie and Kevin spent the night making up for lost time. Her expanding caseload, Horace's corpse, Joe's reinstatement, and finally Gary's death, it all took a massive toll on her. Though a clear path forward eluded her and an air of limbo seemed to hang over her life, she could finally, at long last, unleash her emotions. Kevin gave her space to grieve Gary Maxwell, and waited patiently for her signal to be a shoulder she could cry on.

Kevin arrived at her hotel with an armful of greasy, unimaginative Kung Pao beef and pork fried rice. Jackie lounged in black yoga pants and a gray top, she greeted him wearing no makeup and puffy red eyes. Kevin finished a long bike ride after work and was, as he put it, "sweaty and disgusting." Jackie remembered that she loved his scent, something about his surging testosterone and sweat-slick hair always made her knees weak. She wept off and on as they nibbled at the spread, until she finally kissed him. Hard.

Kevin returned the favor and ripped off his shirt. He scooped her in his arms and carried her from the kitchenette to the bed. She couldn't handle all the conflicting emotions and channeled them into sex. This moment held her pent-up emotional release.

He tugged at her stretch pants; she lifted her hips for him. He knelt before her prone body, leaned forward, and kissed his toned stomach.

They had plenty of sex, but she couldn't remember the last time they made love. "It's been so long, Kevin. I think I forgot how this works."

She giggled and he reassured her, "I read a manual; pretty sure your panties need to be someplace else right now."

He expertly slid them off, her head fell back and her eyes closed. He alternated between stripping his shorts off and caressing her thighs; she moaned as his fingers probed her flesh. Within minutes they were locked in an embrace, her legs clamped around his hips as her heels dug into his back. Their rhythmic movement began to rock the bed, the headboard gently rapped against the wall. Unable to restrain her modesty, she began to moan louder. The soft tapping of the headboard turned to audible bangs, her cries turned to primal screams. Kevin's manhood grew with each of her sounds, she shrieked louder with each thrust. As they approached climax, both were lost in the moment and could not control their emotions. With a finishing thrust, Kevin let out a yell as he came. Jackie needed another minute and continued to grind her pelvis against him, Kevin held still to give her the moment she needed. At long last, her body racked over and over as waves of pleasure escaped her. Her hunger seemed endless as she took what she needed from him. Sweating, heaving, and exhausted, she shook as she held Kevin in place, and, for the first time, whispered I-love-yous over and over. They remained locked in the afterglow until her muscles surrendered. She turned away from him, he spooned her, and she held their interlaced fingers against her bare chest.

Kevin lifted his head and whispered in her ear, "Marry me, Jackie."

She didn't miss a beat. "Shut up, doofus. Get the rest of the Chinese food."

Kevin laughed, stood, and crossed the room out of earshot. Jackie whispered to herself, *Yes.*

Chapter 29

Joe arrived at work at six a.m., long before anyone else. He organized his office, reviewed his files, and contemplated how the staff would receive his return. He spied no bagels, no "Welcome Back" signs.

Um, excuse me? I was exonerated, in case you all forgot. I'm the Nelson Mandela up in this bitch. April Fool's is a few days off, but the stiffs in the office have no imagination whatsoever, so a prank this is not.

Joe settled in at his desk, *at least they had the decency to clean the damn place.* Sitting on his chair was a memo from Dave assigning him two interns. Male interns. Winston and Charles. *Thanks a lot, Dave. You freaking homo.*

Staff began to roll in and eyed Joe like a leper. No one frowned or made faces, but there was no mistake they viewed him with suspicion. A few senior prosecutors stopped in to say hello and commiserate about having that rat bastard Maxwell hurl such horrific allegations in open court. They had all had it happen to them, every prosecutor was subject to a Bar complaint or an allegation of misconduct by a hardened criminal at some point in their careers. It just so happened this particular criminal was convicted of murdering the poor guy's wife.

He also happened to be right, but fuck him.

"At least he had the decency to croak, Joe."

"Yeah, yeah, Jimmy. Hope it hurt like hell when he went."

"He's God's judgment now, Joe. Gotta square it with St. Peter."

"Yeah, yeah, Jimmy. Rest his soul and all that nonsense. But serves the adulterous prick right."

"Murderous prick too, Joe."

"Yeah, yeah, Jimmy. Murderous prick."

The women stayed away. The reason for Jackie's transfer was kept confidential, but Joe gathered that office rumors ran through the coffee klatches like a herd of buffalo. The sewing circle managed to harmonize competing and conflicting gossip into a single overarching theory that Joe threatened Jackie, stalked her, slept with her, and broke her heart. The gossip queens declared that Jackie was a prude but also a floozy and probably got what was coming to her. But Joe suspected that most knew Jackie enough to know Joe was at fault for whatever the hell went on.

But he vowed to win the office back. He ordered a hot spread and paid extra for a rush delivery. By the time the office was humming, several steaming trays of eggs, sausage, and potatoes arrived. The deliverymen carrying the wafting breakfast through the office drew everyone's attention. Joe sent an office-wide email offering food in the kitchen as a way to thank everyone for their unyielding support during this difficult time. He sneered as he hit 'send.'

An hour later, more faces popped in Joe's office to say hello and thanks. More and more colleagues expressed solidarity with Joe and offered their own takes on that rotten murdering bastard Maxwell. By lunchtime, the office was back in a predictable rhythm.

***

Two hundred miles away, Nate Washington sat on the bench hearing argument in a nothing case. His mind drifted all the way back to Chicago. Gossip in the Springfield courthouse revolved around Joe Haise' return to work and what a total shitshow the city of Chicago was. People speculated what he did, some defended him as the victim of a smear campaign by a sleazy killer, others told stories of their personal encounters with Joe Haise and how he always seemed a little off.

He stroked his chin and thought about Jackie. She was strong and smart, but Nate knew something that Jackie didn't: Joe Haise was going to kill her. Maybe not today or tomorrow, but soon enough. She was no match for him because she followed the rules and he didn't. It was just a matter of time. And God knew what he would do to her first. Haise lusted after her; Nate knew it. And Joe had enough on Nate to ensure Nate wouldn't stick his neck out to help, lest he get his head chopped off. How the hell was he supposed to help her? She was a dead woman if he did nothing. And if Nate did something that just wounded Joe, they were both dead. He had one shot. *When you come at the king, you best not miss.*

"Let's take a fifteen-minute comfort break!" Nate stood and hustled off the bench. The courtroom personnel and attorneys were surprised but quickly stood and made arrangements. One attorney turned to his client with a shrug. "He's got the robe, he makes the rules."

Nate walked into his chambers and closed the door. He buzzed his clerk, "Cheryl, print out my current case docket and bring it in." A minute later, his confused assistant walked in with a lengthy printout, he thanked her and asked for privacy. He began to scan the contents.

Sentencing next week... no. Motion to suppress hearing next month... Terrorism. No good. Come on, come on. Wait, motion to dismiss hearing in two weeks... Defendant Piper Dark is charged with electronic theft of funds... Overcharged her amorous customers, assumed frisky professionals would be too ashamed to complain... What else, what else... MyFriendsDontKnow.com... Perfect.

Nate summoned the file and spent twenty minutes reviewing it. He told Cheryl to notify the attorneys waiting in court to take an early lunch; court would reconvene in two hours. He poured over the file, memorizing every detail. Ms. Dark was forty-six years old and looked the part of a modern-day saloon Madame. She impressed like a gracefully aging Hollywood star; long, brown hair with just a few gray streaks, crow's feet that only made her more alluring, and a body that declared its owner had a couple of kids but a dynamite personal trainer.

She became popular when she established a revolutionary dating website, primarily for women, that promised three things: proof of income (over two hundred thousand for men, one hundred thousand for women—blue collar men and secretarial women need not apply), a current face and full body pic that met her rigorous subjective beauty standards, and exactly 50/50 member participation for men and women. She also encouraged users to establish a temporary email account and pay via a prepaid Visa giftcard to ensure no unexplained charges on the family credit card.

Where other dating sites could not exist with accurate demographic data on their customers to sell to marketing companies and recurring monthly credit card charges, Piper eschewed that model and left a pile of advertiser money and monthly fees on the table in exchange for a better client experience. It was genius. All of her customers knew every profile they reviewed featured a single person with education and money, was at least an 8.5 on the beauty scale, and enjoyed total anonymity.

Particularly in Chicago, it was like a drug. Yuppie men competed with one another for admission to the site. Mommies having a wine-fueled playdates would all set up profiles together, "just for laughs." Of course, they never deleted them and spent their nights scanning profiles and flirts—naturally, the married ones would have to wait until hubby was asleep.

While promoting her national website from her home in Springfield, Piper did a few interviews about the first time she had an affair, how her late husband understood that she had needs, how their open marriage made the relationship stronger, and even helped their sex life. Nate had his hook.

He stared at the phone and took a deep breath, knowing there was no going back. This call would change things forever. But she was worth it, she didn't deserve to be a part of the sin that stained everyone else in Joe's world, including him; she could be the one decent thing to emerge from this world of shit with her soul intact. He scanned the room and smiled at the ceremonial gavel, his judicial robe, the framed picture of Nate with the President. A tear fell down his cheek as he dialed.

"Dave Dunham, please. Judge Nate Washington calling."

***

Joe was chatting up a new attorney in the narcotics section, lost in conversation, when Dave Dunham walked up.

"See, Kimber, Narcotics isn't really a transferrable skill. Where else will you go if you ever leave here? Now Financial Crimes, think about it. You come work for me, and within five years you could work on Wall Street, the Merc, hell, any financial services firm would throw *piles* of money at you to be their compliance officer."

"Well, I guess I hadn't really thought about it like that, Mr. Haise."

"Please, call me Joe. I love your shoes, by the way. Are those Ferragamo slingback pumps?"

Dave tapped Joe on the shoulder. "Say, Joe, can I steal you for a minute? I need a favor."

"Sure, Dave. Let's talk later, Kimber. Stop by my office anytime."

Dave tried to forget what he heard Joe saying as they walked to his office, it was ambiguous at best and not worth the fight. *Keep it in your pants, Valentino.* Dave closed the door, motioned for Joe to sit, and settled in behind his desk.

"Joe, I received a request from Roz Jeffries in the Central District. It is rather sensitive but they need someone with your skills for a case."

***

Roz waited for Jackie to respond. "Wait, Roz, am I missing something?"

"Nope, you got it right. This request came straight from Judge Washington. You should check your phone, by the way."

Jackie pulled out her cell phone; she missed a text from Nate sent thirty minutes earlier. It read simply, *Trust me, m'Lady. Do what Roz says.*

Jackie looked at Roz and tried to process what she asked her to do.

***

"It will be one-time thing, Joe, in and out. Now, you'll be in close proximity to Jackie Dekker, but I spoke with Roz Jeffries and she and Jackie are both on board, provided you don't go out of your way to initiate any, shall we say, unprofessional contact. Roz assured me you'll get access to whatever you need, but keep your time there brief. No overnights, leave here in the morning, back here by night."

"I see, and what is the case that requires expertise that only I have?"

"Something about a website that was stealing money from customers, a discreet dating site for professionals to hook up. You wrote that article about online scams last year, so this is really in your wheelhouse. If anyone can untangle their internet scheme, it's you. And some of the customers are people of influence, that lady state senator from Danville, a man who is an LDS church elder, that former goalie from the Blackhawks. None of that is public and we want it to stay that way—we need you to keep it discreet. No need to make this any messier than it already is."

"Do their husbands know?" It was as if he didn't hear a word Dunham said.

Dave exhaled and spoke slowly. "I don't know, Joe. I just need you to get this handled quick and quiet and not cause Jackie Dekker any distress while you are at it, okay?"

Joe stood ramrod straight. "You can count on me, Dave. I'll get on it right away."

Dave stood as well. "Great, you have a hearing in two weeks before Judge Washington, your old protégé. File will be here via courier this afternoon."

Joe walked out with his back to Dave and closed the door behind him; they unknowingly mouthed the same word simultaneously.

Jackass.

***

"So, Nate asked you to formally request Dave Dunham to task Joe Haise—I still can't believe this—to come here to prosecute one of our cases? What the hell?"

Roz nodded. "Jackie, Nate asked for a personal favor from me and Dave. He must have a hell of a reason. I don't know what he is thinking, but from this point on, don't talk to anyone. In fact, delete that text and don't reply. Don't call Judge Washington, Haise, Dunham, or anybody."

Jackie did as she was told and left Roz' office in shock. She shambled back to her office and plopped in her chair. *What the hell is Nate doing? Joe Haise here? In our office? He's gonna kill me, for chrissakes. He's gonna freaking kill me.*

Chapter 30

Piper Dark—her real name—grew up in relative anonymity. She was born and raised in Skokie, her father Andrew descended from British royalty and fell for a comely Jewish girl named Sarah. Piper was raised in a rather conservative home—lipstick wasn't forbidden but only whores wore rouge—and inherited one hundred percent of her looks from her Welsh father's side. All the young Jewish boys vied for her attention and they invited her to every bar mitzvah within a hundred miles.

She eventually married a harmless Jewish man named Jacob, moved to a harmless Peoria suburb, worked a harmless job as an IT specialist at her father's harmless company, and had two harmless adorable boys. By the time she turned forty, she fell into a massive mid-life crisis. Jacob could offer her nothing to lift her out of her funk. But during one fateful business trip in Atlanta, she connected with a network architect, which led to drinks in a hotel bar and, eventually, a glorious one-night stand.

Piper confessed her infidelity out of guilt, and further confessed she loved every minute of it. Rather than seek a Jewish Get and a Gentile divorce, Jacob agreed to keep it secret and forgive her. But the flame within Piper became a brush fire and she began sleeping with other men, sometimes in her marital bed when Jacob was out of town. They ultimately agreed that since he wasn't willing to participate in any way, she needed to rent a hotel room when entertaining her gentlemen callers, lest the children find out. Even Jacob conceded her occasional flings always put her in a glorious mood that carried for weeks and actually improved their marriage.

Before anyone in their community discovered the drama right under their noses, Jacob was diagnosed with cancer and passed away a year later. Freed from her suburban shackles, Piper founded a women-centric discreet encounter site and within two years was worth more than all of their friends combined. She came out of the shadows and revealed her job to the world. Her friends and neighbors eyed her warily, but they admired her pluck and since Jacob had passed on, what was the harm?

But an enterprising programmer created a line of code that added a few nondescript charges to random credit cards from female clients who were unlikely to complain, which added another million a year to the bottom line. Once the federal indictment was handed down, Piper became a pariah in the Jewish community, though she still fielded hushed calls at night from friends offering support and asking if people could still sign up for her site. "Asking for a friend," they would say.

Joe thumbed through the file and paused at a sensual photo spread attached to an article containing an interview she did four months earlier. She was regal, with beautiful chestnut eyes and an air of seasoning that entranced him. She had a woman's body, hips that had borne two children but a figure with just enough oomph to give her ass a wiggle. Far from a doe-eyed young wife or a shameful thirty-something harlot, she was a modern, mature sexual being with a clear understanding of what she wanted.

"I have no shame and no apologies. My husband and I had an understanding. I like sex with talented lovers, I never hid this from him and it ultimately made our marriage stronger. Sex is a pleasurable experience, and if a woman isn't having it at home, there is nothing wrong with finding it elsewhere. God forbid a woman reaches age sixty and realizes, 'My God, I missed the last twenty years because I was afraid to tell my husband I had needs. I've wasted my life.' I want to send a message to men out there, 'Your wife wants to sleep with her best guy-friend. Sorry, but it's true. And she still loves you, but let her enjoy life or let her go. Guys, you can get on the bus or get run over.'"

Joe didn't realize he was fully aroused. He slammed a bottle of water to quench his cotton-mouth and adjusted his slacks. After wiping the sweat from his brow, he began making notes. *Clearly they needed me here, this case is far too complex for those rubes in Springfield. I am sure Jackie put in a word for me, she knows my expertise in this area is unmatched.*

The hearing was scheduled just two weeks out, April 15th, and Joe needed to prepare. Piper's lawyer wanted the judge to dismiss the charges, arguing she had no ability to write a program and there was no evidence she directed the code to be inserted, or even knew it was there. Yes, this was right up Joe's alley. And he would be ready. Of course, a meeting with Springfield staff would be required, that simply went without saying. How could the meeting *not* occur? Then he would be walking into court without preparing himself fully. And who goes to court unprepared? Assholes, that's who.

But how to arrange such a meeting? That would take some effort, a skosh of planning, a little bit of strategery, as they say. Joe stood and closed the door to his office; he didn't need staff disrupting him when he was trying to think. He strode to his computer, sat down while sporting a shit-eating grin, and typed.

```
To: Rosalyn Jeffries, US Attorney, Central
Dist. of Illinois
   From: Joseph Haise, Asst. US Attorney
   Re:   United States versus Piper Dark
   Ms. Jeffries -
   As I am sure you know, I have accepted your
request to assume the prosecution of Ms. Dark in
the above referenced matter. You will not regret
your decision to rely on my years of expertise
on delicate matters such as this. I am review-
ing the file you had sent by courier yesterday. I
will need to spend some time at your office going
over a few things with investigators and talk to
some of your staff. If you would have someone
assigned to assist, it would be greatly appreci-
ated. I hope you can accommodate me next week, I
will arrive Friday around 10:00am.
   Yours in Christ,
   Joseph Haise
```

Joe chuckled as he hit 'send.' *Yours in Christ, what the fuck is that? I crack myself up sometimes.*

***

Roz Jeffries hissed, "*Fucking pig*," as she read her email. She had to stop herself from throwing her keyboard across the room. She considered her options, then picked up the phone and dialed Jackie.

"Jackie? It's Roz. Listen, I am gonna send you an email from our best-est buddy. Don't freak out, but he's coming next week. I will assign Jeffrey to assist him."

Through the earpiece, Roz heard the "ding" of her email being received on Jackie's computer. Silence followed for a long moment. Finally, a hesitant voice responded. "Thanks, Roz. I may be sick that day, if that's alright."

"You have that doctor's appointment that day. Very serious. Physician's consult for your sex change."

Jackie laughed in spite of herself. "Thanks Roz, you always know the right thing to say."

Roz typed a clipped response back to Joe Haise.

```
To: Joseph Haise, Asst. US Attorney
From: Rosalyn Jeffries, US Attorney, Central Dist. of Illinois
Re: United States versus Piper Dark
Mr. Haise -
Thank you for your attention to this matter. I will have a staff member, Jeffery Macklemore, assigned to assist. We will see you next Friday.
Yours,
Roz Jeffries
1 Peter 5:8
```

Roz smirked as she sent her response. *Choke on it, asshole.*

***

Joe heard the 'ding' of the arriving message and spun around from his desk to his computer. *Please assign Jackie to assist… Please assign Jackie to assist….*

He opened the message and frowned. No Jackie. He cocked his head at the Bible quotation, then he opened Google, and then he swore.

1 Peter 5:8 - Be sober-minded; be watchful. Your adversary the devil prowls around like a roaring lion, seeking someone to devour.

Joe slapped the top of his monitor. *Bitch.*

Chapter 31

Jackie spent the next week stumbling from meetings, to court hearings, and back to her office. She heard voices and processed information; she managed to offer coherent responses in court and spoke in complete sentences. She did just enough to ensure that no one could sense her preoccupation; after all, a multiple murder suspect was coming to town to look through her files (fact not in dispute), rifle her desk (more likely than not), and steal her goddamn socks (call it uncharged relevant conduct).

She knew Kevin was ready, willing, and able to offer his support. She knew he was desperate to help her through whatever crisis befalls her. And she knew that he was hoping she'd say "yes" to his marriage proposal.

A cute, sexy guy that is also nice, educated, has no kids or psycho ex, and worships the ugly hotel shag carpeting that I walk on? What the hell am I waiting for? A hotter guy? A richer guy?

But Joe was coming back, and despite Kevin's gallant intentions, Jackie knew Joe Haise would slit his throat and curse him for bleeding all over his knife. Kevin had no idea who he was dealing with.

No, Joe would murder Kevin just because he is sleeping with me and defiling his prized pedestal ornament. If he saw us together? Holy Jesus, it would get bloody. No, I have to. I'm gonna do it. He'll hate me for it, but I won't get another person killed.

She kept Kevin at bay for days, but her resolve weakened late on Wednesday night, thirty-six hours before the Dark Lord would appear in her building. *What the fuck were you thinking, Nate? How could you do this to me?*

She removed a few leftover beers from the fridge, drank them in rapid succession, and dialed her boyfriend-slash-wannabe fiancé.

"Kevin, hey. It's me."

"Hey babe, miss you. It's been days. Can I see you tomorrow night?

I was thinking we could—"

She wiped tears from her eyes. "No, you can't."

He paused, "Wait, are you alright? You don't sound so good."

"No, no I'm not. I can't see you. At all."

Kevin's confusion was evident. "Wait, you mean for a while or forever?"

"I don't know. This case, the next few weeks. I just…just… I can't see you. That's it."

"Whoa, hold on a minute. What the hell is going on? This is crazy, I'm coming over."

"No! Don't you dare! If you come here, I'll scream until they call the cops. Just stay the hell away from me!"

"Jackie, you aren't making any—"

She ended the call, shut off her phone, and threw it across the room.

Her sleep was disrupted, her nightmares were reminiscent of what she'd gone through three months ago in Chicago. Her sociopath of an ex-boss, her sense of being stalked, the doubts and then the certainty, the whole goddamn enchilada was right back on the menu. Weight loss, ulcers, and vivid hallucinations were next if she didn't fix this mess soon.

She made it to Thursday morning before the crying jags began. She managed to stay in her office and keep it from her colleagues, but Roz popped her head in and read her like a book.

"Jackie, that flu bug must have bit you, best to head home and stay there until Monday."

She nodded somberly. "Yeah, thanks Roz. I just gotta get my files in order first."

"All right, but you don't need to prove yourself to me or anyone around here. Everyone's skin is crawling and the secretaries all had to Rochambeau to see who would get stuck being his support staff. We are your friends here, hon. Now get the hell outta here."

Jackie wanted to hug the entire office; she never had colleagues like this. She shut down her computer and went back to the hotel. Apartment hunting was on the weekend's agenda, but she was in no mood and Uncle Sam would have to foot the bill for another week.

She breezed past the flirtatious clerk with her head down and sunglasses on; she couldn't deal right then and just wanted to get to her room. She threw her purse on a chair, kicked off her heels, and left her clothes in a heap at the foot of the bed. She curled up on top of the comforter with a pint of raspberry sherbet and bottle of wine and, for the first time all day, turned on her cell phone. No messages from Kevin. He hadn't called or texted since she shut him down a week ago, save for a single emoji he sent of a bouquet of flowers, she responded with one of a crying girl. This continued every night since. An emoji of flowers, an emoji of a crying girl. Eight o'clock on the dot. She dreaded the day he would stop.

She began to track the clock. Seven fifty, ten more minutes. A sip of wine, a spoonful of sherbet. Seven fifty-five. A gulp of wine, a scoop of sherbet. Seven fifty-eight, her phone dinged. She scrambled to respond. It was from an unlisted number. *Did Kevin get a new phone?*

She opened the app, her blood ran cold.

Just like old times.

Her breathing stopped and she stared at the message. She needed to run. She needed her pistol. She needed Kevin. On cue one minute later, a text arrived: bouquet emoji. She wanted to reach rough the phone and kiss him. But not until His Highness got out of town, and her life, for good. No way she would put Kevin in jeopardy at this point. She responded with three crying girl icons, and one of a couple kissing. He responded with a pizza icon followed by a question mark.

She paused, then typed her first words to him in over a week.

Not just yet.

He responded with a smiley face and then went silent. Jackie quickly polished off the wine and considered the mess she was in.

He's coming, he is going to be so pissed when I'm not there tomorrow. What would he do then? I know what he would do and say if I am in the room with him. But he is going to come looking for me. He may already know where I am staying. No, he already knows where I am right now. So goddamn predictable. I can't keep this up. I can't keep running from this psycho. What am I supposed to do? Something unpredictable. So what can I do that would upend his world?

She had an epiphany. *Nate. Why the hell am I wondering what I am supposed to do? Nate's already done that. Ok, now we are getting somewhere. Nate put Joe here for a reason. For a case assigned to Nate's courtroom. I just have to make sure I don't screw up whatever he has in mind. And I have to figure it out without talking to Nate. Ok, screw this self-pity baloney.*

Jackie threw the blankets off and hopped out of bed. Though she was pretty hammered—the wine went down so nice—she had the better part of her wits about her. She grabbed the revolver from the nightstand, holding it gave her a sense of strength.

She spun the chamber and snapped it back in place. *Ok, Norman Bates, let's play.*

Chapter 32

Spring was knocking on the door and the sun woke up a little earlier each day. Central Illinois in the spring is pretty damn nice. On this morning, Roz Jeffries rolled in to the office at eight o'clock and nearly dropped her coffee when she saw Jackie stroll past her on her way to the kitchen.

"Jackie? What the hell are you doing here? I thought you were—"

"Feeling great, Roz. Listen, can you have me assigned to second chair the Piper Dark matter? I think Jeffrey has enough to do."

Roz looked around to make sure no one was eavesdropping. "Jackie, we talked about this. I don't understand. Why?"

Jackie lowered her voice. "Because screw him, that's why. I'm not going to let him chase me out of another office, no way. This is where I make my stand."

A sly grin crossed Roz' lips. "That's my girl."

Jackie had been stalking around the office since a quarter to six in the morning. She needed to prep the file and get ready, mentally and tactically. She commandeered the small conference room and arranged the furniture just so. As the clocked ticked down, she settled in the conference room and began drumming a pencil on the table. She slowed her breathing as she heard Ruth's voice pierce the silence, echoing down the hall.

"You are all set up in our conference room down here, Mr. Haise. Kitchen is behind you; there is usually a pot of coffee on. Bathroom's on the other side."

Then she heard the familiar urban guttural accent; it sent shivers down her spine. *Here we go, girl. Game time.*

"Thank you so much, Ruth. I understand I've been assigned a young man named Jeffrey to assist me. If he is too busy, I could make do with an old acquaintance from Chicago—"

She saw him turn the corner; he stepped into the conference room and stopped dead in his tracks. Jackie Dekker stood before him smiling from ear to ear. She wore suede pumps, nude stockings, and a tan skirt that rested far enough above the knee that any federal judge would find her in contempt if she wore it in court. She topped it off with a tissue thin-ivory blouse with an extra button open at the cleavage. Her hair stylist gave her a cascading side-swept style that wouldn't be out of place on the red carpet. If she was shooting for unpredictable, she nailed it.

"Jackie! You look, I mean, Jackie! So good to, um, see you."

He warily extended his sweaty palm; she playfully slapped it aside. "Give me a hug, Joe. It's been too long."

She gave him a full-on embrace and made sure to linger a half-second longer than anything socially appropriate. By the time she released her grip, his forehead was damp with sweat.

She knew Joe couldn't find a proper word if he had runway lights and a radar, but Jackie spoke confidently and stole the moment. "Thanks, Ruth. Can you bring Mr. Haise here a cup of coffee? Black, if I recall correctly. Joe, please sit and we can go over the file. Hearing is next week."

Even Ruth seemed to be thrown off-kilter, Jackie's demeanor floored her. She hesitated, muttered, "um, sure," and slipped out.

Joe set his briefcase down, removed a legal pad, and fumbled for a pen while trying to make small talk.

"Things seem nice here. You know Chicago is just so, you know… Gosh, where is my pen?"

He finally sat, Jackie made sure she sat around the corner of the table, but she eased the chair close to him and spun in his direction. She then sat and demonstrably crossed one creamy leg over the other; Joe wasn't even cool enough to sneak a peek. He locked in and was mesmerized.

"Joe. This file is so boring; we could nail it in our sleep. Now, we both know why you were tasked here."

He couldn't peel his eyes of her figure. "We do?" He finally looked up and caught her gaze. She donned a coy expression; the come-hither look threw him off entirely.

Ruth entered with a cup of coffee at that precise moment. Joe whipped his head around looking at Ruth, looking at the mug of coffee, looking at Jackie's legs. But Jackie never took her eyes off Joe, her gaze drilled a hole through Joe's head, she didn't so much as blink.

"Thanks, Ruth. Careful Joe, wouldn't want to burn your tongue."

He took a too-large sip and nearly spit it out. "You said something about…something. Why I'm here. So, why am I here?"

"You're here, silly, because your expertise is required. And I am so glad you stopped by. I have a wonderful career here, I couldn't be happier."

"Well, you know, we could always use you in Chicago. I have some great ideas—"

"Now, now. I appreciate it Joe, but I am thrilled to be here in Springfield. Once we get through the motion to dismiss next week, I suspect I won't see you or the Chicago '*gang*'"—she made air-quotes for emphasis—"for quite some time. Maybe ever."

Joe looked as if he was trying desperately to assume some kind of control over the interaction. "Well, you know, Jackie, our districts should work together more than we have been. After all, you and I really do have a rapport together."

Jackie threw her head back and laughed. "Rapport! Yes, of course we do, Joe. You are always so funny." She offered a playful toe-kick to his shin; he nearly passed out.

She placed her elbows on the table and leaned forward, offering him a clear view of a couple of Springfield's finest. "Listen, you really don't need me here today. Why don't you review the notes, one of the FBI field agents is stopping by, their office is just down the way and he should be here shortly. But I'll see you next week at the hearing. We can talk for five minutes before court, should be very routine. Now don't get up, hon. I have to run."

She pushed back and stood, gave a playful squeeze to his hand, and glided her fingers along his arm and up to his shoulder as she strode out of the room. She walked past her office, grabbed her jacket, and hustled out of the building. She was back at the hotel and changing clothes within minutes.

***

Joe was dripping sweat, but he couldn't remove his blazer lest he display his armpit puddles. He was flustered and spent the first half hour staring mindlessly at the file and running through the entire encounter in his mind. He was not as aroused as he should have been; rather, he was enraged that she seemed to get the best of him. What should have been a Philip Marlowe-esque back-and-forth between the leggy dame and the hard-boiled tough guy instead resembled Charlie Brown laying on the grass while Lucy walked away laughing with the football tucked under her arm.

Goddamn it. I got rolled. I need to step up my game. She's the one who needs my help, not the other way around. Fucking hell.

He gathered himself and began with his case prep. He met with the lead agent, typed up some notes for the hearing, and finally had the agent sign an affidavit as an attachment to the motion response. By one o'clock, he was ready to go. He packed up and stood, Ruth was waiting in the doorway.

"All finished here, Mr. Haise?"

"Yes, thank you Ruth. I wanted to say goodbye to a few people before I go. I wonder if—"

"She's gone. Had a meeting off site. I'll show you out."

And that was that. She was gone, baby, gone. He couldn't even smell her perfume anymore. It went all too fast.

Next week. I'll be ready next week, I already know what I'm going to do. She won't see it coming. Wear that outfit again, you little tease. I dare you.

Chapter 33

Joe spent the weekend stewing around his Libertyville home. She bested him, no two ways about it. By late Saturday night, he was fit to be tied.

She fucking invites me there, she asks for my help, then she comes off as some two-bit floozy? What the fuck is that? She is a certifiable cock-tease dressed all prim and proper, might as well be a nun in a merrywidow for chrissakes. I'm not getting any of that and she goddamn well knows it. So why did she even—?

Joe paused, then he began to chuckle.

Nate. Fucking Nate. Jackie didn't invite me there, Nate did. How else could I have ended up in Springfield? Ah, now I get it. She's trying to keep me off-balance. He and Jackie cooked up something, they are gonna try to bury me. But I've got Nate by the fellas, he can't burn me without taking himself down…oh, Nate, you scheming little shit.

Joe put on a pot of coffee and stared out the window. This will take some maneuvering. He had less than seventy-two hours to prepare; nine a.m. Tuesday morning, the whole smash was going down. He wasn't sure how Nate would do it, but putting them all in the same courtroom was a pretty good start.

I'd need a gun, alibi, gotta remove the motive somehow…nope, I'd be the first suspect if he disappeared. Shit, shit, shit. That won't work, could he have an accident? It would be too suspicious. He has to make the first move, I can't do anything first, the timing isn't right. Unless he chose the easy way out. Yes, that could work, but I have to lay the groundwork.

Joe sat in front of his computer and took a stab at a suicide note using words only Nate would write. *But to whom would Nate address it? That poof he was banging? Grammy Washington? Nope, sure as shit, he would address it to Jackie. Okay, they used to talk in the obnoxious Olde England horseshit he used in emails to her that accidentally fell into my lap. Gotta make up some that.*

In order to write in Nate's hand, he'd have to write in Nate's voice. He'd have to use that old thyme bullshit back-and-forth Nate did with Jackie. Years ago, Tina took Joe to a Renaissance Fair in East Jesus, Wisconsin. It was held in a large field in farm country; he recalled parking on the grass and walking a quarter mile in the dirt to the festival area. There were tents and games and people in costumes laughing and yelling things that he couldn't understand. A bunch of people playing ukuleles and flutes paraded around in clothes that would get them killed if they stepped foot on the South Side of Chicago. A fat neckbeard dressed like King Henry mowed on a turkey leg and lots of women with huge cans walked around in low-cut dresses. Tina had fun, Joe wanted to punch literally everyone he saw. He searched his memory bank for stray words and phrases they used.

M'lady, it is whilst I, consumed with shame and a heavy heart, that I doth have a penultimate flagon of meade and shuffle off this mortal coil.

Joe pushed back from the keyboard. *Fuck. This isn't going to be easy.* He paused that task and prepped an email to Dave Dunham. He would have to send it at just the right time.

***

Jackie spent the weekend preparing as well. *I bested Joe Haise, but it won't happen twice. He is going to be ready next time. Hell, he may even know what Nate is up to better than me.*

The Piper Dark matter was a simple motion hearing to determine if she could continue to be charged with benefitting from a line of computer code she didn't write. Of course, she could; even though someone else had the virtual gun and mask, she was the getaway driver on the information superhighway.

She laid out her clothes, memorized the legal arguments to assist the esteemed psychopath Joe Haise, and tried to figure out what was going to happen. Jackie hated being the clueless one in the room, but Nate was always so cryptic about his past with Joe and no one was tipping their hand either. She was just along for the ride.

***

Nate told his partner Ernest that he needed alone time to prepare for a big hearing and would take his dinner in the den. He offered an emotionless compliment on the meal before slipping away with his plate. Ernest argued a little but let it go. He noticed that Nate had been distant lately; he surmised work must've been dragging him down. Perhaps a getaway weekend next month would help right the ship.

The Honorable Judge Washington sat alone in his locked study staring at a picture of his grandmother beaming with her arm around Nate at his investiture, the ceremony when he was sworn in to the bench. She was so proud. Tears streamed down his cheeks, she would be so disappointed.

Monday came and went. Nate endured a few hearings with a thousand-yard stare. The clerks, even the attorneys noticed he was distant, lost in his thoughts. They didn't know he made a phone call to a reporter during a recess.

***

Joe paced around his Chicago office like a caged animal. He was amped. He drafted an email to his boss, Dave Dunham. Tomorrow's hearing started at nine o'clock sharp, his email would go out at eight fifty-five. Whatever was going to happen, he needed to prep for any eventuality. He withdrew a Glock from a case under his bed. He hoped he wouldn't need it. By Tuesday morning, *D-Day*, Joe rose early and got on the road. He arrived early and drove around town to kill time.

***

Jackie kept her office door closed. The entire staff could sense her unease, but only Roz knew why: her underling was voluntarily going toe-to-toe with a homicidal maniac. Jackie wasn't sure what Nate was up to, he just hoped Joe Haise wasn't any smarter than she was about it. That night, Jackie slept fitfully. She and Kevin exchanged their emojis the night before—at least she had that. She rose well before the alarm and dressed in her going-to-court clothes: navy blue suit, slacks, and an ivory blouse. She sped to the office and sat at her desk watching the clock.

***

Nate rose and wore his best gray suit, sky-blue French cuff shirt with cufflinks he received from Ernest on their anniversary. He managed tough days in his life, nights when sleep eluded him. The pep McDowell prosecution was a roller coaster of emotions; the feeling of uncertainty while announcing, "The prosecution rests." The unease watching the defense's case, learning for the first time where your mistakes were. Then the gut-wrenching wait for a verdict. The euphoria. Then the night before sentencing, when he discovered a mistake. The wave of panic while contemplating, *Is my career over?* Then a lifeline from the last person he expected: Joe Haise. But this was different. Nate was at peace, finally. He checked himself in the mirror, nodded at the reflection in an act of reassurance, and shut out the light. He kissed a sleeping Ernest and whispered, *I love you.* He was out the door.

***

Joe walked through the parking lot and paused at the front door of the courthouse. He pulled out his cell phone and activated his email application. He opened his draft folder, doubled checked the text to Dave Dunham, and hit send. *I hope to Christ I'm right.*

***

One minute to nine, Jackie and Joe arrived at the courtroom door together from opposite directions. There was no witty banter, no gamesmanship. Joe opened the door for her, she accepted the gesture with a nod and they filed in. They both spied a figure sitting in the back they both recognized, Jerry Sloan, a reporter from the Chicago Trib. Right here in River City. Notebook in hand.

Jackie looked quizzically, Joe mouthed, "What are you doing here?"

Sloan looked as confused as they were; he shrugged and cocked his head as if to say, "Your guess is as good as mine."

They settled in at counsel table, Joe pulled out Jackie's chair for her, she sat without comment. They simultaneously nodded across the room to Piper Dark and her attorney; she was dressed in a black pinstripe blazer and skirt and was every bit as striking as the numerous magazine articles said she was. But today, she and her attorney were almost an afterthought in this awful little play.

Joe and Jackie sat stoically, not a word spoken between them. Jackie was sweating, careful not to let Joe notice her discomfort. He was even more nervous than she was, though the great Joe Haise would never let anyone see such a display of mortality. They stared dead straight ahead and waited.

The clerk eased her chair back and announced, "All rise!"

The courtroom attendants stood. Nate Washington emerged; Jackie could tell right away something was wrong. Her best friend wouldn't meet her gaze.

Nate bellowed, "Be seated. I see we have a motion from the defense on this matter. I've read the briefs. Mr. Styles, would you like to be heard?"

The defense attorney, a fifty-something sole practitioner, nodded and launched into his prepared speech. His reputation around town was that of a capable advocate and he was smart enough to know his motion was a dog.

He wrapped up and Nate nodded to Joe for his response. Joe carefully explained the law, pointing to the FBI agent's affidavit in his response brief, and asked the court to dismiss the motion. Jackie recalled that Joe, crazier than a shithouse rat, is still a pretty damn good lawyer.

Nate thanked the parties for their efforts and denied the motion, mainly for the reasons Joe offered. Piper put her head down, but her attorney was unfazed. The attorneys began to pack up their materials when Nate spoke.

"Now that I've ruled on this matter, I have something else to say."

The attorneys froze and settled back in their chairs. Jackie felt a lump in her throat. *Nate, Nate, what are you doing?*

Joe Haise squeezed his prize fountain pen. *Nate, Nate, you little fuck, what are you doing?*

Jerry Sloan re-opened his notepad and leaned forward in his seat.

Nate's voice wavered as he spoke. "Ladies and gentlemen, I donned this robe because of my dedication to the practice of law. I donned this robe because I worked hard for it. And I donned this robe because I lied. And an innocent man suffered because of it."

Jackie's jaw went slack. So did Joe's. Jerry Sloan couldn't write fast enough.

"My last case in the US Attorney's office, I prosecuted a noteworthy matter involving Illinois State Senator Pep McDowell. I missed something, something small but crucial. It would have proved the Senator innocent. Or at least not guilty. And you, Mr. Haise, my former supervisor, helped me cover it up."

Joe winced. *You motherfucker. You are a dead man.*

Jackie gasped. *Oh Jesus, Nate. Don't do this.*

"I don't deserve this robe, and Senator McDowell doesn't deserve the conviction he received. And you, Mr. Haise, for all the evil you did, all the bodies of all your victims, all the evidence you fabricated, you are the Devil incarnate. Maybe I can't prove your deeds, but I hope that reporter follows the trail of the dead and the government puts a needle in your arm. We are adjourned."

Nate hustled off the bench, no one bothered to stand. Joe and Jackie sat back in their chairs and said nothing for what seemed an eternity. The court reporter, who dutifully took down every word in her Stenotype, was practically assaulted by Jerry Sloan as he sprinted through the well and threw a business card at her, demanding a transcript of the hearing.

Nate Washington threw his career, and his life, in the garbage. Jackie finally looked at Joe. "What did you do? What the hell did you do?"

Joe ran his fingers over the suicide note in his jacket pocket. He would have to act quickly. He needed to slip out, announcing his concern for his friend and former protégé, and get to Nate's chambers. The untraceable gun rested in the bottom of his briefcase, ready to go. Fortunately for Joe, prosecutors are allowed to bypass courthouse security. Joe cleared his throat. "Well, obviously—"

A muffled gunshot echoed through the walls. Jackie was the first one up and through the courtroom toward the judge's chambers. Joe trailed, followed by Sloan. The clerk managed to hit the panic button as the sound of screams from the court reporter reverberated behind them.

Jackie arrived at the chamber door first, but paused just long enough for Joe to shove her aside, turn the knob, and burst through first. The honorable Nate Washington evidently removed his judicial robe, sat at his desk, and shot himself through the head. Jackie screamed as Joe held her back. Others joined in the hallway. More screams. Marshals arrived and pushed everyone back.

Jackie's knees buckled and she sobbed. "No! No, no, no! God, no!" She cried so hard she didn't notice Joe Haise was holding her up.

Joe was too shocked to enjoy holding Jackie that close. But his intellect was as sharp as ever. *No need to kill him, I guess. Saved me the cost of a bullet. Bit of good luck, there.*

Minutes later, the hallway was flooded. Roz Jeffries arrived and Joe dutifully handed a grieving Jackie Dekker over to her wordlessly. He then waved Jerry Sloan over, who practically tripped he was so desperate to arrive at his prime subject.

"Mr. Haise! What do you have to say about the allegations Judge Washington made before his death? Do you have a comment, sir?"

Joe straightened his jacket and smoothed his tie. "Judge Washington was an old friend and my former protégée. His death is a shock to us all. But his mind was clearly deteriorating. Why, just before court, he caught me in the hallway and was mumbling about nonsensical things, black helicopters, radio waves in his teeth, conspiracies involving the whole judicial system, and so forth. I was so concerned about his well-being that I sent an email to my supervisor, US Attorney David Dunham, immediately before court, advising that I felt Judge Washington was unwell and had a tenuous grip on reality. I assume Judge Washington summoned you here, Mr. Sloan, so that you could bear witness to, what I can only describe as, the rantings of a madman. I only hope you will be delicate when you write about his public mental breakdown."

Sloan flipped pages rapidly, making sure to catch every word, verbatim. "This email, can I have a copy?"

"Of course, just contact Mr. Dunham. He can forward you a copy.

I was quite detailed in my comments. And one more thing, I can't believe Judge Washington mishandled the McDowell case. I supervised him, along with many others, so I hope my trust in Nate wasn't misplaced. But I make this pledge to you: I will personally review that file to make sure he engaged in no shenanigans in the prosecution. Justice must prevail."

Jesus, I can't believe that shit worked. Way to go, Nate.

"Any other comments, Mr. Haise?"

Joe suppressed a smile. "I just hope whoever takes his place on the bench will do honor to my good friend Nate's memory."

Chapter 34

Jackie stared at the ceiling of her hotel room, still wearing her suit. Her phone rang constantly, but she rejected the calls. She sent a text to Kevin telling him that she was fine. She promised she would call him later to talk about what happened. She cried, more for Nate's memory than her friend. *He will only be remembered for fixing a case and killing himself in shame. Joe forced his hand; I just know it.*

Jackie would never be able to think of Nate the same way again. *No one is what they appear to be, everyone has a little dirt.*

Her train of thought was broken by her phone showing a text from an unlisted number.

I think we should meet.

She texted back. *Marriott bar, fifteen minutes.*

There was no sense going someplace else, Joe knew where she was staying. Hell, he was probably sitting in the parking lot. She grabbed her purse, slipped the revolver inside, and headed downstairs.

Joe arrived exactly fifteen minutes later to find Jackie exchanging an empty martini glass for a full one. He saddled up next to her and ordered a mineral water. She refused to turn her head.

"Hell of a day, Jackie."

She nodded after taking a healthy sip. "Did you help Nate fix the McDowell case?"

He paused and smiled. "Testing…testing…1, 2, 3. Anyone there?"

"I'm not wired, Joe, I'm drunk."

"Well, then this is all hypothetical, just in case. And you should never ask a question like that. But, yes. Yes, I did."

She shook her head. "You corrupted him, you sonofabitch."

Joe offered a *tsk, tsk*. "Now, now. He is—was—a grown man who made his own choices, he just couldn't live with them. That robe was always a little too heavy for Nate."

"Don't talk about him like that; I don't like his name in your mouth."

He nodded thoughtfully. "Fair enough."

Jackie forced herself to set aside her grief for the moment and think like a lawyer, it was a well-worn sweater she could always slip on. It always fit. "Are you going to vacate McDowell's conviction?"

He furrowed his brow. "Dunno. Maybe. I'll pin it on Nate, either way. I'm clean in all this. I'm ahead of the game, always have been."

"I'm sure you thought this through. Nice comments to Jerry Sloan, by the way. How the hell did you know Nate would shoot himself?"

Joe smiled and shook his head in disbelief. "I didn't. Would have had to do it myself. So, this was something of an unexpected benefit. Hell, I had a plan worked out and everything. Foolproof even, if I do say so myself. I had a sample of his handwriting, a suicide note, and a copy of Black Inches magazine. Just needed an opening."

"Fuck you." Jackie nearly bottomed her glass. "You're going to kill me, aren't you?"

Joe's jaw nearly hit the floor. He wouldn't face her, but the wound was evident. "Kill you? Are you mad? I've been your—what do you all it?—silent protector. Who got you the job when you were a lowly intern? Who gave you those good cases? And who saved your life from that Horace DJ Eldrod whatever-the-hell his name was?"

She half-turned. "You? That was you?"

Joe nodded smartly. "Naturally. He was stalking you for days. I think you owe me some appreciation for that one."

Jackie buried her drink and signaled the barkeep for another, snatching it and taking a healthy gulp before he could even place it on the bar. "You're a sucking fycho, I mean a fucking psycho. And your career is in the shit."

He let out a chuckle. "Don't think so. In fact, I may end up in Nate's seat."

She nearly choked on her drink. "You? On the bench? Your reputation is garbage and the courthouse gossip is that you killed your wife. Not to mention how many more bodies are in your cellar. Forget it, Joe. The President will never even nominate your sorry ass."

Joe pulled out two crisp twenties and laid them on the bar. "You let me worry about that." He gathered his coat, bent down, and whispered in her ear, "And I don't bury them in my cellar, silly. That's a rookie mistake." He turned and walked out the door.

Jackie thought briefly of shooting him in the back; in her state, it was a warm and comfy fantasy. But she was no killer, and he was right. He's always one step ahead.

***

The media crush was like nothing Springfield had ever seen. Hordes of reporters swarmed the region. Prosecutors, court staff, even grizzled locals gathered in coffee shops endured relentless questions right in the middle of their Moons Over My Hammy.

Did you ever see the judge around town? Do you think gay men face additional scrutiny in rural Illinois? How many other mentally ill professionals are in the federal judiciary?

Wearing pajamas and gulping cold beer in front of the TV at the hotel, Jackie and Kevin collectively snorted over that last tag line. Jackie surfed for more news coverage. Seeing herself on national television, albeit without being interviewed—the Department of Justice had a person for that—was rather intoxicating. *Maybe profile isn't so bad, after all.*

"So, wait, Joe had nothing to do with this? Really? Nate shooting himself, I mean."

Jackie shook her head. "Nope, he was probably going to kill Nate himself and stage it as a suicide, but Nate saved him the hassle." Jackie clicked her tongue out the side of her mouth. "Lucky sonofabitch."

He placed his hand on her knee. "You need to cry? Or laugh? Because I can't tell."

"I am all cried out, Romeo. I loved Nate, and I *thought* I knew him. But cooking the McDowell case? I never would have guessed he was involved. He wasn't as pure and wonderful as I hoped."

"Nobody is, hon. So, what happens now? Joe's done, right? I mean, that shit about him becoming a federal judge... Never happen, right?"

Jackie was still, lost in thought. *Federal judge...Federal judge...so how precisely would he go about—*

"Jackie?"

She snapped back to reality. "Hmm? Oh, well, knowing Joe Haise, I think he's probably thought three moves ahead."

Kevin scooted across the bed and intertwined his legs with hers. "Because if he ended up with Nate's seat, he'd get to see you, like, every day. You can't let that happen."

Jackie drew a smile across her lips. "Well, we can't have that, now, can we?"

Chapter 35

A week passed and Jackie struggled to make it through each day. The entire courthouse was silenced, cases were pushed off, trials postponed, Peoria's docket was sent to Springfield. She just had to make it to the memorial service. Just that far and everything would get better afterwards. Ten days after Nate's death, Jackie donned her black pantsuit and somberly shuffled into the funeral home. It was a muted affair, only a handful of friends and family. The press was still in full gear: *Was this Haise fellow, whose wife was brutally murdered by her lover years earlier, unfairly smeared by a raving lunatic? Will former State Senator McDowell have his conviction overturned?* It was a bounty of sleaze. She remained composed during the service; Kevin held her close, but he felt emotional distance between them. He wondered if she didn't need him to keep her standing straight anymore.

Asked to say a few words about his former colleague, Dave Dunham considered that Nate claimed to have fixed a case under his watch and politely declined, sending flowers instead. Jackie couldn't blame him; it was a fair compromise under the circumstances.

Two weeks after the funeral, Jackie started hearing rumors that the state Bar was vetting a small handful of people for Nate's seat. Many federal judgeships are unofficially categorized. A particular Circuit Court of Appeals seat is set aside for someone from a particular state, a District Court seat is for a lawyer with a criminal law background, etc. But the theme for all the candidates for this seat was the same: a white-collar practitioner from Chicago.

***

If Joe wanted to be on that short list, he needed to act fast. He sent an anonymous email to a reporter suggesting that Chicago Assistant US Attorney Joe Haise, yes, *that* Joe Haise, was being vetted by the Illinois Bar for the seat. The reporter dutifully called Joe who cryptically stated he is honored just to be considered and that having to endure the many slanderous accusations that come with a career in criminal prosecution left him with a coat of armor for a bruising Senate confirmation battle that seems to happen with every nominee these days. Beyond that, he "…would have no comment about who contacted me to initiate the vetting process. *If* I was contacted, that is."

The Chicago Trib ran an article a few days later discussing the vacancy. A few individuals were not serious players, but insiders whispered their names to reporters as a favor. One candidate was a retired Congressman, a good and reliable party soldier who needed to boost his profile for the Sunday talk-show circuit before his next book launch. Another candidate was a nationally-known female black civil rights lawyer whose rumored candidacy was really payback for keeping her mouth shut when she caught a highly-placed White House staffer getting a blowjob from a Portuguese hooker.

But the remaining names being floated were all Chicago white-collar crime experts. Jonathan Wickman, a law professor who literally wrote every white-collar federal statute of significance for the last ten years, and a personal attorney for the President of the United States, was a strong candidate. But everyone knew he would have to take an 80% pay cut and would probably politely decline; Mrs. Wickman enjoyed both the country club and yacht club memberships in Chicago and would prefer not to relocate to central Illinois. And of course, the esteemed Joe Haise, whose only real crime was being unfairly maligned by, well, everybody that knew him well.

***

"Jackie, he isn't going to get it. I mean, come on."

Jackie massaged her temples and exhaled. "Roz, nothing about him shocks me anymore. No, I think he has the inside track on this one."

"He didn't really admit that he smoked DJ Elrod whatever, did he?"

"Yeah Roz, he did. But do NOT tell anyone. If he thinks you know…."

"Yeah, then I'm going to have an accident."

"Bingo. Sweet Jesus, part of me just wants to run away. In a perfect world—"

Her ringing phone interrupted them. Roz waved her off and walked out of Jackie's office, closing the door behind her.

She scooped the receiver, leaned back in her chair, and shut her eyes. "Financial Crimes, Jackie Dekker."

She rubbed the bridge of her nose and uttered, "Mm hmm" several times. She gradually opened her eyes. "I'm sorry, what is your name?"

The voice on the other end spoke, she shook her head. "Wait, I just need to process…when did you want to meet?"

***

Two days later, Joe sat quietly in the waiting room elegant leather Chesterfield chair, occasionally dusting off his slacks and checking his wristwatch. The trappings were exactly what he would expect. Cherry wood desks and bookcases, floral-print wallpaper, and the slight aroma of rose petals in the air. A spread of high-power reading materials—Forbes, Wall Street Journal, Donald Trump's Biography—suggested his host was someone who knew what it took to be successful. Joe thought, under different circumstances, they could've been kindred spirits.

***

Jackie sat in a stained gray fabric chair with plastic armrests. The entire waiting room reeked like armpits. A small coffee table in front of her held an old copy of Us Weekly and a single used Kleenex. The caramel-skinned receptionist wore a low-cut top displaying a tattoo strategically placed just above her illogically-large breasts that read "Fuck Tha Police." She cracked her gum while she texted on her phone, occasionally chatting but refusing to look up.

"What was your name again? 'Cause he didn't tell me shit."

"Dekker, Jackie Dekker. I have an appointment at two o'clock."

She finally paused to look Jackie up and down. She grimaced at the pretty blonde white girl in a skirt and blazer sitting across from her, Jackie knew this woman didn't care a whit for her from the moment she walked in. She returned to texting while making idle conversation.

"Yeah, I don't know what appointments come in sometimes, he doesn't tell me what's up, you know? Like, one time, we had a dude come in, and he was a playa-type brother and super fucked up, and this skinny white bitch with him was all—"

The desk phone rang; she casually finished sending a text before answering.

***

The stern, fifty-something receptionist occasionally peered over her bifocals, attempting to convey her distaste for an unscheduled visitor demanding her boss' time. The bun in her hair was tight enough to compress carbon into diamonds and her resting bitch face could stop traffic. But her guest didn't seem the least bit fazed by her rehearsed glare.

"I'm sorry, what was this about again, Mister...*Hay-zee?*"

"It's Haise, pronounced like 'lays.'"

Heh heh, 'lays.'

"And it's something of a delicate personal matter, ma'am. His daughter and I are...acquainted."

She looked disgusted and returned to her computer. Her phone rang. She quickly picked up the receiver, covered her mouth, and spoke in a hushed tone.

***

"Yeah, Miss Dexter is here. You want to see her, or what?"

Jackie uncrossed her legs. She could hear rushed movement behind the door as footsteps hustled across the floor. The door to the adjoining office flew open and a slightly disheveled fifty-something man greeted her.

His brown polyester tie rested poorly over a dull white shirt with a small coffee stain near the breast pocket. Her host flashed a mouthful of yellow teeth and was trailed by a cloud of cigarette smoke, but his enthusiasm was genuine.

"Ms. Dekker? Whew, so glad to meet you at long last! I'm Lou Dalrymple, welcome to Dalrymple and Streicher."

***

Her whispers were barely audible. "*No sir, he doesn't have an appoint-...says he's a Federal prosecutor...said it's personal...something about your daughter....*"

She quietly hung up the receiver and forced a smile.

"Mr. Haise, Senator Druckleford will see you now."

***

"I'm sorry, Mr. Dalrymple, I only recall you sent an email on behalf of Gary Maxwell about conditions of confinement. I wasn't aware your… representation…went beyond that."

"Well, Ms. Dekker, I like to think we are a full-service law firm here. And estate planning is just one of our many talents. I spent time with Mr. Maxwell in the hospital before he passed and we spoke often by phone. He was really quite intelligent."

Jackie tried to look indifferent, but she deduced the ambulance-chaser behind the desk was undressing her with his eyes and making no attempt to be discreet about it. "I'm sorry, I don't understand what this has to do with me." Jackie felt the germs from this hellhole creeping into her bloodstream and beating the holy hell out of her immune system. *I'm going to be sick after this, I just know it.*

"Oh, I thought someone would have told you by now. Well, as you know, this Joe Haise character settled a wrongful death claim against Mr. Maxwell, and then of course the divorce from his wife Veronica, all of that left Mr. Maxwell with just a fraction of his pre-incarceration estate. Of course, a fraction to him may be different to you and me."

"Oh, well, I honestly didn't know. We never talked about those things. What exactly are you saying?"

"Well, his wish was that you would use this specific bequest to assist wrongfully incarcerated persons get proper legal representation. Like the Innocence Project that Scheck and Neufeld started. But it's really your call. You have complete discretion over the matter." He leaned forward and placed his hands on the desk. "Ms. Dekker, after arranging for his children to be cared for, Mr. Maxwell left you the bulk of his remaining assets, just a whisker shy of two-point-nine million dollars."

***

"Senator, so glad you could make five minutes for me. I know you are a busy man."

"Yes, well, thank you, Mr. Haise. And I recall your name, so if you are here about the judgeship in Springfield, I can tell you that I have many people interested and we have a commission that typically helps sift and winnow the candidates."

"I'm sure you do, but I think I should be on the top of that list, Senator, and I'd like to see you make that happen."

The elder statesman, a lion of the Senate and one of the most powerful men in the most powerful political body in the world, was short on patience. "And why would I do that for someone who, to be frank, hasn't done anything for the party or my campaign, as far as anyone can tell."

Joe displayed a shit-eating grin. "I am sure your daughter, Amy, would appreciate it, Senator."

***

Jackie walked out on wobbly legs, shambled to her car, and collapsed in the driver's seat.

Oh my god, I'm rich. Student loans, I am done with student loans. I can quit my job, right? Is that enough to live on? I don't know. What do I do? I can get the hell out of here, that's for sure. Springfield was nice for a while, but it is a constant drumbeat of right-wing radio and NRA bumper stickers, no decent arts scene, and lousy takeout. Holy cow, I can do anything. Start a non-profit? Do I start my own Innocence Project?

Or maybe I go work for an existing group one for a dollar a year? I can do anything! And Joe Haise can kiss my back pocket. Holy cow, this little town is in my rearview.

She peeled out of the lot, cranked the radio, and opened the windows. The spring breeze blew through her hair and she smiled, a genuine blissful got-the-world-by-the-tail smile, her first in ages. It was ten minutes before she realized something she never considered: *Kevin.*

Chapter 36

Joe Haise sat in his office in Chicago and grinned as he scanned the web for news. Day after day, legal bloggers gradually separated the wheat from the chaff of judicial nominees, and Joe remained on every shrinking short list. The comments section of one website, thankfully for Joe only a few courthouse insiders ever read, contained one blistering screed.

Joe Haise, like the turd circling the bowl no matter how many times you flush, keeps floating to the top. He is a total creeper! My roommate works with him and he is a sleaze. Always looking at her tits. And they all say he offed his wife but no one knows for sure.

He sneered and casually looked out his office window at the workers buzzing in the pit, trying to determine who was the blabbermouth. *Hmm, female employee, living with a roommate. Should be a short list.* Joe vowed to get to that later.

Well, if Senator Druckleford wants me to continue to suffer from amnesia about his acrobatic daughter with an affinity for Burberry pocketbooks, none of this should matter.

***

"I don't know, Kevin. My life is kind of a mess right now. I mean, my tormentor is about to become a federal judge, meaning I will have to appear in front of him every week, practically. And now, with this money, I just can't stay here. I gotta go." She didn't tell him that it was a full ten minutes after learning about her massive inheritance before he even entered her mind.

Kevin responded little, nodding periodically and sipping wine as they sat in muted conversation at the hotel bar. At long last, he spoke.

"You're right, you can't stay here. You have to go. Someplace else, *anyplace* else. Are you going to start a nonprofit or join an existing one?"

She constantly bounced her knee and fidgeted with her glass. "I don't know just yet, I think I have to decide to go somewhere I can do the most good. I really do want to help make sure people don't get screwed by the law."

He swallowed hard. "Do you want me to come with you?"

After a pregnant pause, she looked at him with watery eyes and spoke with a lump in her throat. "I don't know. I can't ask you to quit your job and follow me to wherever and watch Judge Judy all day. You have a great job here. Do they need bike paths in Washington, DC? Or Manhattan? Or Portland? It's not fair, I know. I'm sorry this all happened."

He reached over and brushed the tear from her cheek. "It's not your fault. Tell you what, let's get drunk, order some lousy pizza, and fool around all night. And when life finally takes you someplace far from here, we can hope it's a place that is in desperate need of more bike paths."

She laughed, wiped the rest of her tears away and kissed him. "If only we'd met in some other time, in some other place, Kevin." *Fate sucks, sometimes.*

Hours later, they lay exhausted and sweaty in the moonlight, sheets draped over their naked bodies. He finally spoke.

"Where do you think you'll end up? If you had to guess right now."

Jackie chuckled. "Honestly? I think I already know. I figured it out when you were tearing my panties off."

"Glad I wasn't able to distract your steel-trap mind, dear. My ego just took another nice downgrade. Okay, Murder She Wrote, don't keep me in suspense. Where is it?"

Jackie sat up, letting the sheet fall and exposing her breasts to Kevin, who always smiled when she did that. It was her favorite move.

She brushed her hair back and grinned. "Back to Chicago. I just need to do something first."

***

Joe stopped doing anything remotely resembling work. He spent his days checking the news and his phone to see when it would be official. *If anyone deserves this, it's me. For all I suffered, with my wife being brutally murdered and all, the universe owes me.*

He pivoted back to his computer to finish the first draft of his investiture speech when his cellphone chirped, announcing the arrival of a text.

Exchequer Bar. Fifteen minutes.

Joe's heart stopped. *It's her, oh my.* He grabbed a bottle of cologne from his desk, slapped on a generous amount and sprinted for the door. He rushed past his secretary, leaving a kerosene fog in his wake, and barked about an "offsite business meeting." He promised that he'd be back in an hour.

He burst in to the east-side Chicago tavern, his eyes adjusted to the dark and darted back and forth in search of her. Sitting alone at the bar, sipping wine, was the love of his life, Jackie Dekker.

He tried to play it cool, sidling up next to her and ordered a mineral water with lemon.

"Jackie, looking beautiful as always."

She nodded. "Joe. So, I hear you are in line for Nate's seat."

He relaxed and threw out a dismissive hand. "Oh, well, it's an honor just to be considered. There are so many qualified applicants and if I am fortunate enough to—"

"Cut the shit. Remember, I know you."

Joe smiled. "It's a lock. And I can't wait to have you appear before me. I will strive to be fair and objective, but I won't deny that if you show a little leg, you may find me more receptive to your motions. You see, Jackie, when any red-blooded man—"

"I want your old job. Head of Financial Crimes here in Chicago. And I want you to get it for me."

Joe nearly spit out his water. "What? First of all, you are too inexperienced. People work ten years for a position like that."

"Well, I will just have to earn the trust of staff, won't I? My problem, not yours."

"And why the hell would I deliberately put you that far away from me?"

"Because if you don't, Joe, I'll go public."

Joe laughed. "About Tina? Nice try. Jammer Franks considered it, Maxwell tried it, hell, even Nate gave it a go. Didn't work out so well for any of them."

"Nope, Joe, not about Tina. About me."

"You? What did I do to you? That you can prove, I mean."

She set down her glass and looked him dead in the eye. "Well, there was the time you tried to rape me in your office."

Joe nearly screamed. "Rape?" A few curious faces looked up, but quickly went back to their business. He spoke in a forced whisper, "*I never touched you!*"

"I don't care, and neither will anyone else. I'll stage a hunger protest at your Senate confirmation hearing. I will come off as a raving psycho if I have to. You recall Anita Hill, and Thomas had the White House backing him. Whatever it is that you have on Senator Druckleford—yeah, everyone knows he is shilling for you—he isn't going to support you in the face of the heat I will bring down. You have a pencil-thin grip on the seat, and I can break it in two."

"You'll come off as a loon and lose your job, Jackie. I promise that."

She smiled. "Don't care, I don't need it any more. I recently came into some money. Like, a *lot* of money. I'm talking 'fuck you' money."

Joe furrowed his brow. "How the hell did you…Maxwell. Bloody hell, I never thought of that. His will is in probate, isn't it? Damn it, missed that one. How much?"

She looked at him and winked. "Three mil, tax-free. I've decided to help those wrongly accused get justice, and what better place than running a division at the US Attorney's Office? Dave Dunham loves me, I'm sure he'd be on board. You just need to have your Senator friend make a call."

Joe nodded; he had to respect her. "Well played, Jackie. I think I was a better mentor for you than I ever intended."

She finished her wine and stood. "Do we have an arrangement?"

Joe tipped his glass to her. "We do. I'll take care of it. Enjoy my job, it isn't easy, you know. Are you sure you are up to it?"

She sauntered past him towards the door. "I think so; I already have my first case picked out. Remember the Pep McDowell case?"

Chapter 37

Six months later, things seemed to shake out as they should. Jackie managed to get Joe's old job in her old division, thanks to glowing recommendations from United States Senator Jed Druckleford, US Attorney Dave Dunham and, ironically, the Honorable Joseph Haise. Jackie saw to it that her office vacated Pep McDowell's conviction, though Joe's fingerprints were nowhere to be found on the false prosecution, naturally. Jackie quickly resumed her old life, albeit this time in a tastefully appointed three-bedroom condo on the lake. While eating spectacular Korean takeout late one night, overlooking the lights of the city from the private walk-out off her modern industrial bedroom, she realized she was home. *I'm a city girl, no two ways about it.*

Jackie made an anonymous donation to Her Way, a charity started by the late Tina Haise that offered inner city Chicago girls the chance to spend a few weeks in the summer in the safety of a summer camp in northern Wisconsin. The charity struggled to remain afloat after she died. Although it never employed more than two people, Tina was a charmer and could get people to open their checkbooks and keep the camp going. Donations dried up after Tina's death, but Jackie's efforts would guarantee that the charity would survive. She organized a black-tie fundraiser with the goal of making it an annual affair to ensure Tina's memory would endure. All the big shots in Chicago's legal community attended; when silk stocking firms learned the new chief federal white-collar prosecutor was involved in the charity, they all sponsored a table. Jackie even put together a video presentation of pictures and video clips of Tina that left half the room in tears.

Joe Haise did not attend due to prior commitments.

He was downstate, in his new grand Lake Camelot home located just outside Peoria, standing naked in his living room ironing a floor-length black robe.

The well-to-do Central Illinois community embraced their newest resident. Joe was unlike the previous judge, and the local Women's Auxiliary reminded him of that fact quite often. "The black fellow was one of the *gays*, you know, Mr. Haise." Joe frequently referred to the baby Jesus and his love of firearms and the local celebrity golf pro offered Joe admission to the most exclusive country club in the area. A white, conservative Christian-sounding male was just what this area needed, he was assured.

He spent his evenings checking the web for the quality of local "talent;" it wasn't anything close to Chicago. He'd have to travel if he wanted professional company of one sort or another. At least his neighbor across the fence had an easily-guessed and powerful Wi-Fi signal that snuck—uninvited—into his home. *Trespassing rat fuck.*

One autumn night, after having tee-many-Martoonis with her new staff from the office, Jackie made it home around midnight. She stripped down, threw on a nightshirt, and sat on her balcony enjoying the late evening breeze off the lake. Then she did something she repeatedly vowed in the daylight to never do: texted Kevin past midnight when she was hammered.

Hey you, how are you doing? I had booze and wanted to say hello.

Minutes passed before her phone finally dinged. *Did you drive, Madame Prosecutor?*

She laughed. *No smartass, everyone Ubers here. You should be here, too.*

:) Maybe one day.

Jackie pouted. *Boo! Why not tomorrow? Have you met somebody else already? Hahaha.* She wasn't really joking with her last question.

No one here wants to date a nerd like me. And I think you have your plate full for now. Besides, you know you only miss me after midnight and when you've been drinking, lol.

Jackie sighed. *No, Kevin, I miss you all the time. I just can't ducking slay it. Slay it. SAY it. Damn autocorrect.*

Go to bed, naughty girl. Our (bike) paths will cross again someday soon. Get it? Maybe Lake Shore Drive needs some new bikepaths.

She laughed. *Okay, but I may text you again some night after too much Sangria.*

Sounds like a plan. Take care, girl. - Like, Kevin

She donned a melancholy smile, shut down her phone, and looked out over the cars cruising along Lake Shore Drive.

CPSIA information can be obtained
at www.ICGtesting.com
Printed in the USA
LVHW052013290620
659286LV00002B/513